A Full Life

John F Burdett

Published in 2009 by YouWriteOn.com

Published by YouWriteOn.com

For Jeremy
who started it

Contents

Ministry

Easter

Commissioning the Church

Introduction

Foreword

This book has been written in the hope that it will be read by people who are unconvinced that God exists, or that Jesus was his Son, but who nevertheless are interested in the Bible and wonder if it has any relevance to life in the 21st century.

But it is also written for people who believe in God and his Son, in the hope that it will strengthen their belief in the relevance of the Bible, not only to life in general but also, more importantly, to their own lives.

I have attempted to keep these two aims separate. The first part of each chapter is intended for the non-believer who is not interested in the lessons that Christian believers derive from a particular passage in the New Testament. The second part is devoted to a consideration of the passage from a Christian perspective.

My attempt has not been entirely successful. My own beliefs have inevitably crept in and non-believers will, of course, realise that although they themselves may not believe in God, the Bible is about people who did.

What Version?

Throughout this book there are references to passages in the Bible, but there isn't room to print them in full, so you'll find it useful (though not essential) to have a copy of the Bible available. If you haven't got a Bible and don't want to buy one, go to www.biblegateway.com, where you can look up the references in a wide variety of versions. The Bible is so large that anyone approaching it for the first time will find it daunting, and may find it difficult to decide what version to choose. The Authorised Version (sometimes called the King James Version) is unrivalled for the beauty of its language, but it's not always easy to understand and you may prefer one of the modern translations. Some of them have a habit of paraphrasing the text, which can lead to inaccuracies, so if you want to study a passage in any depth it's a good idea to compare several versions. In the church that I go to we use the New International Version, which is one of the best, but if you want down-to-earth, colloquial language you may be happier with the Good News Bible.

Historicity

I wonder what your immediate reaction is to the words "Once upon a time ..." . If you're like me your feeling's perhaps of pleasure, perhaps a little excitement, or at least anticipation, and possibly, strangely enough, a feeling of security. Perhaps for those of us who were lucky enough to be read to or told bedtime stories the association is with the warmth and comfort and security of bedtime. Whatever the reason, most of us like being told stories and the story-teller can often convey messages and make points far more effectively and memorably than a lecturer or a speech-maker or a preacher.

Most (though not all) people would agree that the story of the creation in the first chapter of Genesis isn't historically true. Nor, for that matter, is the story of the Garden of Eden in the second chapter. But though historical truth is important, it isn't the only kind of truth and a myth can, and often does, express a kind of truth which can't be expressed in historical terms. For example, if we say that the story of the Fall is a myth we're not denying its truth, we're saying that its truth lies deeper than the kind of historical truth that depends on dates and documentary evidence.

There is, I believe, archaeological evidence of a major flood in Sumerian times, but I think we can safely assume that the story of Noah and the ark isn't literally true. Nor is the story of the Tower of Babel. And when you remember that the version of the first five books of the Bible that has come down to us probably dates from 600 years after the time of Moses, I think you'd be justified in wondering if some of the other stories and characters in the first part of the Bible are historically accurate. But though we may doubt their historical accuracy, that's no reason for suggesting that they've got nothing to teach us both about human nature and about our relationship with God.

The same applies when we come to the New Testament. The writers of the Gospels weren't interested in history as we know it. Mark must have been familiar with a large number of stories about Jesus, and he presents us with a selection of them. He must have chosen the ones he thought were especially relevant to the circumstances of his own community, and arranged and presented them so as to bring out the truths about Jesus' life and work that he felt it was most vital that people should grasp.

Matthew took Mark's Gospel and expanded and arranged it for the benefit of people with a sound knowledge of the Old Testament. He gave his Gospel a more specifically Jewish flavour.

Luke used Mark's Gospel, too, and combined it with other sources. His Gospel seems to have been intended for general publication, and his object seems to have been to tell the Roman authorities the truth about the Christian religion and to show that Christians didn't present any sort of threat to good order.

John tells us why he wrote his Gospel. Right at the very end he says: "Now Jesus did many other signs in the presence of the disciples, which are not written in this book; but these are written that you may believe that Jesus is the Christ, the Son of God, and that believing you may have life in his name." And although John's Gospel is very different from the others, that statement could apply equally well to all four Gospels.

None of the evangelists is trying to write a biography. They tell us nothing about Jesus' appearance, physique or health. It doesn't even occur to them to tell us whether or not he was married! They're not primarily interested in a bald description of what took place. What they want to convey to us is what was going on in the context of what took place. Not how something happened, but why.

The stories at the beginning of Matthew's and Luke's Gospels are like the stories at the beginning of the Old Testament: myths – stories conveying truth but not technically historical truth.

The events surrounding the birth of Jesus are described in some of the world's best-known stories. People who know little or nothing else about the Bible know the story of the shepherds and the wise men.

They are lovely stories. But if we're honest, there must always be a suspicion that it didn't really happen like that – that Luke made up the story of the shepherds and their journey to Bethlehem; and for that matter that the wise men from the east never really existed – that Matthew made up the story about the star that they saw and their journey to Bethlehem and the gifts that they offered to the infant Jesus.

In fact there are people who say that it couldn't have happened like that; for example, that Luke got his dates wrong. But when someone tells us a story, whether it's the Three Bears or the Good Samaritan, we don't say: "I don't believe that really happened." We take pleasure in the story and perhaps learn a lesson from it. And the same applies to the stories surrounding the birth of Jesus. Whether or not they're historically accurate is quite unimportant. We just know that our lives are richer for them, and the people who say it couldn't have happened like that are missing the point.

About Time

We're liable to think of the Bible as a sombre, gold-edged book, written a long time ago in an archaic language – a book that has nothing to do with or say to people in the 21st century; a book written so long ago that the various parts of it and the events that they describe all seem to date from the same period. But just for a little while let's bring the Bible forward by 1,900 years:

Abraham probably lived during the 2nd century CE. The Jewish Exodus from Egypt probably took place in the 7th century. The books Genesis and Exodus as we know them were written at about the time of the Norman Conquest, though they are based on much earlier work. Isaiah and Hosea lived in the 12th century. The exile to Babylon took place in the 14th century. Most of the Old Testament had been completed by the end of the 15th century, but the Book of Daniel, though it purports to have been written by Daniel himself during the exile, was written in about 1735. Palestine was absorbed into the Roman Empire in 1837, when Pompey captured Jerusalem.

Jesus was born in the late 1890s and executed in about 1930. Paul started writing his letters to the young churches in 1948 – less than 20 years after the crucifixion – and went on writing until his own execution in 1967.

The first Gospel – Mark's – was written between 1965 and 1970. Matthew's was written a few years later. Luke wrote his Gospel and the Acts of the Apostles between 1980 and 1985. John's Gospel is due out any time now. There are still a lot of people alive who are old enough to have met Jesus and heard him teaching.

Following a Jewish revolt, Jerusalem was destroyed in 1970.

Incarnation

Annunciation

Luke 1: 26 – 38

One of the wonders of the Old Testament is the way in which it shows us the development of the Jews' perception and understanding of the nature of God. When we first hear of them the Jews think of the Lord as being the greatest of all gods, with whom they have a special relationship and whom alone they worship, but still only one god among many. And then gradually their ideas begin to change. The process is slow and irregular, sometimes in quite small steps, occasionally in enormous explosions of revelation, and it's brought about mainly through the teaching of the prophets.

Amos sees a basket of figs and a man with a plumb line and realises, what possibly no one had realised before, that Yahweh isn't the god of Israel only. He is God – God of all the world. Hosea's discovery is simple but even more dramatic. He learns that God is love; and he learns it, astonishingly, from his own wife's infidelity. Isaiah foresees the Prince who will rule in peace and justice – as innocent as a child and as mighty as God.

And so the preparation goes on until the Jews are as ready as they'll ever be for the coming of the Messiah.

But the Jews weren't the only people whom God was preparing. Their development was paralleled by what happened to the Greeks, though it's interesting to notice the differences.

The Greeks really broke through into history when they defeated the Persians at the battle of Marathon, long after the Jews had returned from exile. At that time they genuinely worshipped a whole lot of gods and goddesses like Zeus, Apollo, Hera, Aphrodite and so on, all of whom were simply personifications of natural forces and human impulses. They were primitive people's attempt to explain the world in which they found themselves. But a religion of this sort rapidly becomes incredible in the face of natural science, and natural science was a thing the Greeks were remarkably good at. They came to realise that thunder wasn't the result of Zeus being angry and that if the crops failed it wasn't because someone had upset Demeter.

And so while the Jews increased their understanding of Yahweh, the Greeks lost faith in their gods and gradually, under the influence of the philosophers, who in some ways were the equivalent of the Hebrew prophets, they came to believe that there was one celestial Being above and beyond all creation. Someone in Athens even put up an altar to him – The Unknown God.

And so the people were prepared for the coming of the Christ. But the conditions for his coming had to be right, too.

It was only after the battle of Actium in 31 BC that Rome annexed Egypt and the emperor Augustus was able to establish the peace and stability that were to last for 300 years and more. But in the biggest empire the world had ever known good communications were essential – as essential as they were for the spread of the Gospel. Without good communications efficient administration would be impossible; and without good communications the Gospel would wither at its source.

And so the Romans set about building their road system, driving them past all obstacles; and when they'd finished it was as if – as Isaiah put it – every valley had been exalted and every mountain and hill had been made low as they made a straight highway for our God.

That's not to say, of course, that no one ever travelled before the coming of the Romans (of course they did) or that travel was never dangerous afterwards; but before the establishment of the empire, journeys were difficult and hazardous. The road from Jerusalem to Jericho wasn't the only one where you were liable to be mugged.

But given good roads, what better place could there be to start from than Jerusalem? On the main land routes between Rome, Alexandria and the valley of the Euphrates, it stood, in effect, at the junction between Europe, Asia and Africa. Jerusalem could almost be called the communications centre of the world. But not for long, because in 70 AD it was destroyed by Titus.

So there was only that short period of 100 years between the battle of Actium and the destruction of Jerusalem for the communications system to be established and for the Church to be founded and to develop sufficiently to be able to spread from Jerusalem.

Precise timing was essential, but everything was ready. The Jews were at a peak of expectation, the Greeks were looking for a God to fill the vacuum left by the discredited Olympians, the Romans with their usual efficiency had taken care of the logistics. Everything was ready for an event so awe-inspiring as to overshadow even the magnificence of the preparations. Everything was ready, except for one vital link on which the whole stupendous plan depended – the willing cooperation of one young country girl. And so the Archangel Gabriel goes and asks for her help, and the hosts of heaven wait breathlessly for her reply . . . "I am the Lord's servant. May it be to me as you have said." And heaven breathes again.

That's all ancient history now. What's it got to do with us?

Non-believers stop here

In all this the Christian can see that God is working his purpose out, although amid all our worries and preoccupations it may be hard for us to see what that purpose is – as hard, perhaps, as it was for the Roman soldier dying at Actium, or the British slave building the road that we know as the A1, or the Jewish carpenter hanging on a cross. But to achieve his purpose God relies on the willing cooperation of people like us, now just as much as he did for the greatest purpose of all. God proposes, but Man disposes. It really is up to us.

Nativity
Luke 2: 1 – 7

It had all started about nine months previously when a young country girl had an unexpected visit from a most unusual person and she accepted the greatest of all vocations. She was to be the mother of the Son of God.

From then on, like any pregnant woman, she must have been continually thinking and planning ahead. And she must have been constantly wondering where the holy child would be born. As she looked round the room behind the carpenter's shop with its homely, familiar furniture, it must have seemed incredible that it should be there. But where else could it be? Perhaps the angel would come back and tell her. But the months passed slowly, the routine of life went on and still there was no sign – just housework and cooking and shopping – her contentment marred only by the knowledge that people were gossiping behind her back about how she'd got herself pregnant. But at last the time drew near.

And then almost at the last moment she had to make a dreadful choice. Joseph had to go to Bethlehem. There was no need for her to go too and she'd be well looked after if she stayed in Nazareth, but she couldn't be separated from Joseph just at that time, and anyway she'd like her baby to be born in David's village. So she took the risk and made the difficult journey.

When they got to Bethlehem it was packed. There were very few women about, because only men were compelled to go and register. And there were men everywhere – in the streets and in the pubs, talking and singing and shouting.

But there was still no sign of the angel – no guidance about the birth of the baby. Had it all been a dream nine months ago? But if so, where did the baby come from? It was a depressing and worrying time as Joseph hurried from one house to another looking for shelter. All he could find was a stable behind a pub, and there that night the child was born.

Exhausted with the journey and her labour she heard no angels' songs – only the raucous noise from the street outside. It was dark and she was lonely with no friends near except her dear Joseph. Joseph sat on the tail of a cart swinging his legs, feeling a bit helpless and inadequate as husbands often do, but too tense to settle down to sleep. He looked at his wife with overflowing love and pride and he looked at the baby with something like awe, but still with that nagging, ugly suspicion.

The hours went slowly by. The shouting and singing in the streets died down. Now all was quiet and cold and dark and rather gloomy. And then.... footsteps. The stable door opened and a group of rough-looking men came in. Joseph started forward to bar their way, but they hadn't come to take but to bring. To bring surely the strangest gift ever known. For by their kneeling before the manger, by their story of what they'd seen and heard on the hillside they brought the assurance that Gabriel's words had come true.

Think what their visit meant to Mary. The darkness in her mind was changed to radiant light. It was true! God hadn't forgotten. She hadn't been fooling herself. The incredible had happened and the babe in the manger was indeed the Christ. It was the shepherds who had brought that light. That was their supreme gift as they talked about the multitude of the Heavenly host and the song they'd sung of glory and peace.

And the shepherds went away, glorifying and praising God. And everyone who heard them wondered at the story that they told. They came, they saw, and they went away to tell other people – the first preachers of the Gospel.

Even if that story is in some (perhaps many) respects inaccurate, there's no doubt that Jesus was born in Palestine within a few years of the date that Luke indicates. That is an historical fact; we're dealing with Jesus Christ here, not Father Christmas.

Non-believers stop here

The Christmas story tells us that God comes to this world in and through ordinary people. He comes to people like the shepherds – people who are neither wise nor wealthy, people at the bottom of the social ladder, people who have nothing to give but their love. He comes to people like Joseph, who trust him against all the odds. He comes to the people who throng our city centres at Christmas time, celebrating something, they hardly know what, but still enfolded in God's love.

And he comes to people like Mary – people who have the insight to discern God's will and the courage to accept it – people who are homeless, lonely, dispirited as she was.

But there's more to it than that, because just as God needed Mary's willing cooperation before his will could be done – before Jesus could come down to earth and be born in Bethlehem – so today God needs our cooperation so that he can come to people who are poor or homeless or lonely or in despair. But if we have faith and are ready to do his will he can and does come.

So, like the shepherds, 'let us go even unto Bethlehem and see this thing which is come to pass'; and then let's return home praising and blessing God for all the things which at Christmas time we hear and see and do.

Epiphany

Matthew 2: 1 - 12

The sequel to the story of the birth of Jesus and of the shepherds who found him lying in a manger is almost as well known – the coming of the wise men. There could hardly have been a greater contrast between these two groups of men. But for that very reason it's important to think of their journeys to Bethlehem not as two different stories but as two episodes of the same story.

The good news came to the shepherds as a sudden, unexpected revelation when the angel of the Lord came upon them and the glory of the Lord shone round about them. The shepherds were poor and ignorant. Their faith was simple, unreasoning, unquestioning; the kind of faith that results in a warm, emotional worship from the heart.

The wise men's worship was quite different. They weren't poor, ignorant countrymen. They were rich, educated, cosmopolitan. Their worship was based not on a sudden revelation but on patient, scientific research. Theirs was a reasoning, questioning faith and the worship that followed it was worship of the mind. They probably came from Persia (modern Iran or Iraq) whose wise men were famous for their knowledge of astronomy, and they must have believed in the influence of the stars on human destiny. So when the star appeared they looked for its meaning, and they may have found it in literature left behind after the Jewish captivity. Perhaps it was something like the verse in the Book of Numbers which says: "A star shall come forth out of Jacob and a sceptre shall rise out of Israel." I wonder why Matthew didn't quote that. He was always anxious to show how the events of the New Testament fulfilled the prophecies of the Old.

And having concluded that the star indicated that a king of Israel had been born the wise men didn't leave it at that. If they'd been content with merely noting the fact they'd have learnt very little. The secret wasn't revealed to them until they'd laboured to find it. They were prepared to back their judgment and to spend time and trouble and money on their search. They had their doubts and perplexities, as I suppose all true scientists do when they're engaged in research. The light failed and they had to ask for the help of other wise men in Jerusalem. Their success came from their scientific training which enabled them to note the phenomenon, and from the scientific method by which they sought out its meaning.

So the shepherds and the wise men came to Bethlehem by very different routes. The shepherds had a sudden revelation and went on the spur of the moment – "Let us now go even unto Bethlehem." The Magi worked it all out carefully and then had to plan a long journey. The shepherds probably brought nothing with them. The Magi brought costly gifts. The shepherds were Jews. The Magi were foreigners. The shepherds went to find a saviour. The Magi went to find a king. But they all found their way to Bethlehem and between them they illustrate the all-embracing nature of Christ's Church and of his command: "You shall love the Lord your God with all your heart and with all your mind." God has given us brains as well as emotions, and he expects us to use them. Jesus always demanded thought from his hearers. That must have been one of the reasons why he spoke to them in parables – to make them think.

Non-believers stop here

It's not given to many of us to receive a sudden, blinding flash of clear, explicit revelation as the shepherds did, but if like the wise men we are prepared to take what has been revealed to us – perhaps in the Christmas story, perhaps in other ways – and to work at it and think about it and pray about it, we too will find the way to Babe of Bethlehem. We've got his own promise of that, because he who is the Way said: "Seek and you shall find." So, as Christmas calls us to lift up our hearts in joyful, unquestioning worship, in the same way the Epiphany calls us to obey our Lord's command to love the Lord our God with all our mind as well as with all our heart. He came to make us whole. He came that we might have life – life in all its fullness, and he asks us to love and serve him with our whole selves. Christmas and the Epiphany aren't two stories, they are one; and we must try for both kinds of worship.

As Paul said in his letter to the Romans: "I implore you by God's mercy to offer your very selves to him: a living sacrifice, dedicated and fit for his acceptance, the worship offered by mind and heart. Then you will be able to discern the will of God and to know what is good, acceptable and perfect."

Boyhood

Luke 2: 21 – 52

Only one of the four Gospel writers – Luke – tells us anything about Jesus' life during the 30 years between his birth and his baptism. Luke describes two incidents – both of them related to Jewish ritual. The first was his circumcision. The story gives us some indication of his family background, because of the sacrifice that his parents brought with them. The Law (Leviticus 12:8) required them to bring a pair of turtle doves or two young pigeons. If they had been richer they would probably have brought a lamb, while if they'd been poorer they would have been allowed to bring a small quantity of flour. We know that Joseph was a carpenter, so we can deduce that Jesus was born into a middle-class family and that his parents were faithful to the Law of Moses.

They have two strange encounters in the Temple. Simeon refers to Jesus as being a light to lighten the Gentiles, foreshadowing the prologue to John's Gospel: "The light shines in the darkness". The reference to the Gentiles was remarkably prescient. It would be a long time before Jewish Christians – let alone the Pharisees – came to accept that the good news of the kingdom of God was for all people, not just for themselves.

But Simeon leaves Mary with a note of warning. He quotes Isaiah: "He will be a stone that causes men to stumble, a rock that makes them fall". He will be a source of strife and controversy, and Mary herself will suffer to see the result of people's rejection of her son.

Mary and Joseph must have been surprised to say the least of it. If you took your infant son to be baptised and two old people talked about him in those terms, what would your reaction be? After the visit of the shepherds in Bethlehem, Luke tells us that Mary treasured up these things and pondered them in her heart. Now she had more to think about. She must have wondered what was in store for both herself and her son.

Perhaps she got some indication twelve years later. It looks as if the family were making a special visit to Jerusalem to celebrate Jesus' Bar Mitzvah. Nazareth is more than 60 miles from Jerusalem, and travelling in a group at the speed of the slowest members of the party, the journey would have taken at least three days each way. So the whole expedition must have lasted at least two weeks. Joseph, with a business to run and a living to earn, would not have been able to take that much time off very often.

Up till now Jesus had probably been just an ordinary small boy. Certainly Luke knew of no earlier incident that he thought worth recording. Now Jesus, without telling anyone, stayed behind when the rest of the party started for home. Fairly typical thoughtless behaviour from a nearly-teenager, one might think. But what was not typical was the way he spent his time while he was on the loose. He went to what must have been the equivalent of university lectures, and he created something of a sensation by his understanding of what he heard. More things for Mary to ponder over. Perhaps she was not greatly surprised when Jesus' whole way of life changed after his baptism in the river Jordan.

25.7.10

O God, you have taught us that all people must be brought to fear you, to love you and to serve you. We pray for the nations of the world that the rich and the strong may support the poor and the weak and that all people may live together peacefully, free from the fear of violence or persecution. We pray for the people who are suffering as a result of events over which they have no control, whether natural or man-made. We remember the members of our armed forces who are putting their own lives at risk on our behalf. Give wisdom to the leaders of all nations that they may understand both the motives and opinions of their opponents and the potential consequences of their own decisions. Lord, in your mercy . . .

O ~~Almighty~~ God, you have promised to hear the prayers of those who ask in faith. We pray for your Church, in all its branches and denominations. We ask for your blessing on Brian our Bishop and on the whole Anglican Communion as it struggles to resolve the sincerely held opposing views of its various branches, remembering that we are all one body in your Son because we all share in one bread. Lord, in your mercy . . .

We give you thanks, O God, for all the good things of this life; for the love of our families and the affection of our friends; for security and harmony; for the work of all the people on whom our comfort depends; for the beauty all round us and for the ability to enjoy it. And we pray for the people who are deprived of these things.

Refugees and all who are homeless. Those who are blind or deaf or housebound or unemployed or in prison. All who live in slums and the ugly places of the world. Help us never to be content with the life which we enjoy until we have done everything in our power and by your grace to help others to share them also.

We pray for all who are ill and for all who need the care and protection of other people, remembering from this congregation

And in a moment of silence we remember the people we know who especially need our prayers. . . . .

Lord, in your mercy . . .

As we pray for those who have died, we remember from this congregation

Grant, O Lord, to both the living and the dead that together we may share in the joy of your Son's resurrection and in his eternal Kingdom.

Merciful Father , accept these prayers for the sake of your Son, our Saviour Jesus Christ.

First Encounters

John the Baptist

Matthew 3 Mark 1: 1 – 11 Luke 3: 1 – 22 John 1: 19 - 34

"John came, baptising in the desert region and preaching a baptism of repentance for the forgiveness of sins." That's the first event recorded in Mark's Gospel. But Luke puts it into context. He's writing for educated Romans, and he must be aware that the stories he's told so far about the birth and childhood of Jesus are likely to be treated as myths. It's time to get down to some historical facts.

He needs to make it clear that the events he's about to describe, although they took place in an obscure and distant province of Rome, were an important part of world history. So without giving us an exact date he gives us a series of clues to indicate when John started his baptising mission. Unfortunately the clues are confused and confusing, but it's probable that John started his work in A.D. 27.

We've got so used to the concept of baptism that we're liable to miss some of the significance of what John was doing. Baptism had never been part of Jewish religious practice. During the century before the birth of Jesus a fairly widespread baptising movement had grown up in Palestine, but it wasn't popular with the religious bureaucrats in Jerusalem, and Luke tells us that the Pharisees and lawyers refused John's baptism. He says that John was in the wilderness until the day of his manifestation to Israel and that the word of God came to him in the wilderness, so it's possible that he was a member of one of the ascetic communities in the neighbourhood of the Dead Sea – perhaps the Essenes.

The elder Pliny refers to a large settlement of Essenes in the area near Qumran, where the Dead Sea Scrolls were found, so the Qumran community may have been Essenes. The Essenes appear to have used baptism, but it seems to have been an extension of the Jewish practice of ceremonial washing before meals – similar to Muslim ritual washing before prayer – rather than an initiation ceremony.

So John's introduction of baptism would have been quite new to most people, which is perhaps why he became known as John the Baptiser. He himself seems to have seen his baptism as only part of his preparation of the people for the coming of the one who was mightier than him. He said: "I baptise you with water for repentance, he will baptise you with Holy Spirit. The reason I came baptising with water was that he might be revealed to Israel."

I wonder if it was a disappointment to him to become known as John the Baptiser. He seems to have thought of himself as primarily a prophet; the last of the prophets. And Jesus agreed with him. He said that John was a prophet and more than a prophet. John pointed away from himself. It wasn't who he was but what he said that mattered. He quoted Malachi and he dressed like Elijah. That may have been because Malachi had said that Elijah would return before the Messiah came. And John quoted Isaiah. He said: "I am the voice of one calling in the desert, 'Make straight the way for the Lord.'"

I suppose for a lot of us, particularly those of us who were brought up on the King James Bible, those lovely verses from the 40th chapter of Isaiah are, so to speak, built into our foundations: "Comfort ye, comfort ye my people, saith your God." We don't remember a time when we weren't familiar with it. And yet its very familiarity tends to conceal from us what the prophet's really saying. We're liable to let the words wash over us without really listening to them. "In the desert prepare the way for the Lord; make straight in the wilderness a highway for our God." Why? If we want to welcome a head of state we decorate our streets, we prepare our towns. Why prepare a highway in the desert? And why prepare a highway for God, who surely doesn't need one?

I suggest that to find the answer we've got to think first not about the highway but about the desert. Because this desert, this wilderness, this lonely place without life is within each one of us. There's a part of each one of us in which there's an absence of contact, a sense of being isolated, alone – sadly or frighteningly or even just boringly alone.

And this is the desert into which and through which the prophet calls us to build a highway for our God – because highways are for communication, communion. The highway into our wilderness will let God into the desert that Christians believe we've shut him out from. It's a desert because we've shut him out from it. And with the communication, the communion, comes the community – the fellowship of the Holy Spirit. That's another phrase that Christians hear so often that we almost forget to listen to it. And this fellowship, this community, involves communion not only with God but with our neighbours. And all this stems from the building of the highway in the wilderness.

But how do you build a highway? If you're lucky you have bulldozers and earth-moving equipment, but for most people in most parts of the world it's a slow, painful process of carrying earth, dragging stones, rolling boulders, chipping away at immovable rocks, getting rid of everything that's in the way. But first you have to decide where you're going – to plan the route, to work out which boulders you've got to shift, which rocks you've got to chip away. You've got to carry out a survey of the route.

And it's the same with the highway in our own wilderness. We have to identify the things that are in the way – that we've got to get rid of. The deliberate sins that we know perfectly well about but we don't want to give up. The sins we're hardly aware of – the thoughtlessness, the lack of sensitivity. The sins we're so used to that we take them for granted because they seem to be part of us as we are.

Looking at all these things is our survey of the route for the highway, and this self-examination is part of what Christians are called upon to do during Advent and Lent as they prepare for Christmas and Easter.

But there's an order, a sequence, of ideas that we have to follow if our highway is going to get to its goal. And that applies in secular life as well as religious matters.

Where health is concerned, for example, we must acknowledge that we're ill before we can accept a cure. We must be ready to receive information before we can profit from it. You probably know the remark: "I've made up my mind, don't confuse me with the facts." We must acknowledge that we're ignorant before we can start to learn.

I recently had a good example of that. I've always been a good theoretical cook. I haven't actually done much cooking, but I know how to go about it – how it ought to be done. But then I attended some cookery classes and realised how little I knew and how much I didn't know. I realised, for example, how important it is to do things in the right order if you're not going to get into the most almighty guddle.

Acknowledgement of need has to come before fulfilment of need. In the same way, repentance must come before faith, and both of them are God's gifts, not something we do for ourselves. By putting John the Baptist at the beginning of their books, all four Gospel writers seem to be saying that we have to begin by thinking about sin and repentance and our need for purification before we can hear the message of Jesus in the right way.

Jesus is all about forgiveness. He proclaims God's final amnesty before his kingdom comes. An invalid is let down through a roof to meet him, and Jesus' first words are: "Your sins are forgiven." He knew that sinners can't save themselves – they can't, in fact, repent unaided – and he spent a lot of his time with people who knew that; people like tax collectors who couldn't escape the guilt of their occupation. But all his rich generosity, all his teaching about God's acceptance of us as we are, would have been lost on us if we hadn't previously heard John's call to repentance.

We have to get into the messy, unsatisfactory business of self-awareness – of regret and sorrow for what we've done or not done, of longing to change and be changed. But we also have to be made to realise that we can't do it on our own. We try to obey John's call to repent and we find that we can't.

But we're not the first people to discover that. Paul said: "Even though the desire to do good is in me, I am not able to do it. I don't do the good I want to do; instead I do the evil that I don't want to do. What a wretched man I am! Who will rescue me from this body of death?" And it's only when we've accepted that – when we've been through the preparation that John called for – that we can see that what Jesus is telling us is good news. We have to be told that we must repent before we can accept the forgiveness of our sins that Jesus offers us.

But repentance means much more than being sorry for our sins – more than just changing our mind. It means a change in our personality, our attitude to life. Repentance involves active acceptance of God's gift of faith. And faith isn't a question of believing what you can't prove. It's trust in the reliability and steadfastness of God. And if we have that trust we can ourselves become steadfast.

As Isaiah put it: "You will keep in perfect peace him whose mind is steadfast, because he trusts in you. Trust in the Lord for ever, for the Lord, the Lord, is the Rock eternal."

It's interesting to see what instructions John the Baptist gave to people who asked his advice. To ordinary people who were blind to the needs of others because of their preoccupation with their own security, John didn't say: "Give away everything you've got." He said: "Don't be selfish. Share what you've got with people who are less fortunate than yourselves." To tax collectors he said: "Don't collect more than is legal." To us he might have said: "Pay what is legal. No fiddling of income tax. No little bits of smuggling on your way home from holidays abroad." To soldiers he said: "Don't try to augment your income at other people's expense."

But we mustn't be too negative about all this. Repentance implies looking back, thinking about our sins and shortcomings. John's instructions were largely negative. But that was perhaps natural, because he knew his Bible. And his Bible was what we now call the Old Testament, and it was dominated by the Ten Commandments, with their repetitive "Thou shalt not". One of the great and joyful contrasts between the Old and New Testaments is the difference between the negative "Thou shalt not" legalism of the Old Testament and the positive "You shall" freedom of the New Testament.

I've counted up the number of times in the Gospels when Jesus is recorded as having said: "Do not". Of course, a lot of them are repeated in more than one Gospel, but the total comes to just over 60. If you cut out things like "Do not be surprised when I say", the number of actual commands is about 55. But what to me, at any rate, was quite unexpected is that 20 of those are repetitions of one or other of two closely related sentences: "Don't be afraid" and "Don't worry".

Jesus' teaching is full of positive statements, typified, of course, by his summary of the Law: "You shall love the Lord, your God with all your heart and mind and soul and strength" and "You shall love your neighbour as yourself". I think it's very significant that on so many occasions when he found it necessary to say: "Don't" his concern was with people's peace of mind: "Don't be afraid, don't worry".

But Christians are followers of a master who took a very positive attitude to life, and his baptism marks a dramatic shift in thinking.

So what positive steps should we take? How are we going to clean up our act? Let's go back to Paul again, and see what he had to say: "Fill your minds with those things that are good and that deserve praise: things that are true, noble, right, pure, lovely and honourable. Think about <u>those</u> things. Rejoice in the Lord always. I'll say it again: Rejoice! The Lord is near. Don't worry about anything, but in all your prayers ask God for what you need, always asking him with a thankful heart. And God's peace, which is far beyond human understanding, will keep your hearts and minds in union with Christ Jesus."

Non-believers stop here

But to go back to our highway. Self-examination is only the beginning. Surveying the route doesn't build the highway. And when we build our highway let's go about it the right way. We're not like a contractor building a motorway from scratch where there was no road before. We've got to repair and rebuild a road that's already there – a road that will lead us to God and to our neighbours, a road that's been neglected and got obstructed through lack of use.

And that's another thing about roads. They need constant attention to keep them open. Some magnificent roads have been built through the deserts of the Middle East, but if they hadn't been constantly maintained great sections of them would have disappeared under the sand long ago. It's not enough just to prepare ourselves for Christmas or Easter. We've got to keep on and on and on, keeping the road open, keeping ourselves open to God by prayer and Bible study, keeping the communications open by the service of God and our neighbours, by the Holy Communion.

But don't let's ever forget that this highway is a dual carriageway. On the one hand it enables us to obey Jesus' command "Come to me." In one sense our whole life is a journey towards God, and perhaps we can think of church buildings as being literally service stations – places where we can have a brief rest, get some refreshment and check our road map to see that we're on the right route. But we have to travel in the opposite direction, too. Jesus said: "Go into all the world" and again we must check our route, work out how we can spread the good news, how we can communicate with other people so that we can bring them too along this highway to our God.

But although all that's important, if we left it at that it would give quite the wrong emphasis. It gives the impression of men and women trying to build their own highway on their own initiative by their own efforts. In fact, of course, the initiative is God's. Jesus has had experience of the wilderness; he knows what it's like to feel totally alone. "My God, my God, why have you forsaken me?" And to those who trudge down the road like the disciples on the way to Emmaus, feeling that their lives have been shattered, that everything that their hopes had been centred on has been taken from them, Jesus himself draws near, even though in their grief they don't recognise him.

So the initiative is his. And he's trodden this road already. He knows the route. He is the way. And at the service station it's he who provides the refreshment: "Come to me all that labour and are heavy laden and I will refresh you." In the Eucharist, the Holy Communion, he offers us the gift of the Holy Spirit who will guide us into all truth because he is the truth. And it's he who brings life to this lifeless desert; he who came so that we might have life – life in all its fullness – because he is the life.

Jesus said: "I am the way, the truth and the life. No one can come to the Father except through me." The highway for our God is his. And I think that's what John the Baptist was getting at.

But what about the people who for all their efforts can find no road and no route along which to build one – people who feel that God has shut himself away from them, who've begun to doubt his very existence? It's a condition in which many of us – perhaps most of us – find ourselves at some time in our lives. When it happens it's up to us to do what we can – to make the best use of the gifts and abilities that God has given us – in the faith that this condition is temporary and that ultimately we'll find our route to him. And do you remember what Milton said about God? "His state is kingly. Thousands at his bidding speed and post o'er land and ocean without rest. They also serve who only stand and wait."

Temptation

Luke 4: 1 – 13, Matthew 4: 1 – 11

"You are my Son, whom I love; with you I am well pleased." Those were the words that Jesus heard as he came up out of the river Jordan after his baptism. They gave him all the assurance that he needed that he was indeed the Son of God. Now he had to work out what that meant for himself, for his ministry, and for the world; and the temptations that Luke tells us that he faced in the desert sprang from very fact that he was the Son of God. "If you are the Son of God, you can do anything. You can do anything you like."

Some people say that the temptation to turn stones into bread was a temptation to satisfy his own hunger, and of course if that were so his motive for doing it would clearly have been self-centred. But I don't think that was the temptation. For one thing he'd gone into the desert voluntarily. If he was hungry he could do what anyone else would do – walk to the nearest village and buy food. But I think that in any case food wouldn't have been a source of great temptation to Jesus. He enjoyed food and drink, but he was a man who didn't set much store by creature comforts, and I don't think hunger would have worried him too much.

A great many country people in Galilee must have been poor almost to the point of starvation, and Jesus would have known that it's not much use talking about spiritual things to a man with an empty stomach. So it would be logical to suggest that the first thing to do would be to use his miraculous powers to feed people, and that after that they'd be in a better state to listen to his teaching. And to a compassionate man feeding the hungry is clearly a good thing to do. Why else do we support Christian Aid?

But, as so often happens, the good was the enemy of the best. Jesus knew that any attempt to feed people in that way would be centred on him as a man. Who would turn stones into bread for them after he'd gone?

Later in his ministry he said: "I am the bread of life", and this first temptation was to substitute earthly bread from Jesus the man, for the bread of heaven, the body of Christ.

In any case, simply to give people food doesn't solve their problems. It makes them economically dependent. They lose their freedom of choice. You'll notice how when governments give aid to Third World countries there are usually strings attached, so that the rich country acquires an export market or a source of cheap imports.

At first sight Jesus' answer to the devil seems strange: "Man shall not live by bread alone, but by every word that proceeds from the mouth of God." But who was it that said: "Give a man a fish and you feed him for a day. Teach a man to fish and you feed him for life."? The Word brings independence, freedom.

The next temptation – to be the absolute ruler of the world's only super-power. Surely the world could only benefit from being ruled by a wise, benevolent dictator. But you've only got to look at our own times to see what chance he would have had of establishing universal peace and justice, and what the attempt would have meant in terms of compromise with evil and corruption – with worshipping the devil.

He'd be the all-conquering Messiah the zealots were waiting for. But any attempt at world conquest and domination would have gone the way of so many revolutions – starting with high ideals, with freedom for everybody, but ending with armies of occupation, secret police, political prisoners, the lot, as he tried to force his will on people.

In Jesus' imagination the scene changes again. He thinks of the huge temple court in Jerusalem at Passover time, seething with a dense mass of pilgrims from all parts of the world. Suddenly, one after another they look up at a figure outlined against the sky on the topmost pinnacle. What a thrill of horror there would be as the figure leaped forward from the tower! But when instead of him crashing to the pavement below, the crowd saw him floating gently to earth, borne up by invisible angels, their horror would turn into delirious fanaticism. Every member of the crowd would be instantly converted and would hail him as the Messiah.

It would compel people to believe in him. He'd have been the centre of attention all right; he'd have been a nine-days' wonder. But it wouldn't have lasted. It would have proved almost nothing. It certainly wouldn't have proved God's love for all people. It would have been an easy way of convincing people, but again it would have been an attack on their freedom.

Jesus saw, and allows us to see, that this was a temptation to do something contrary one of the principles by which God has always governed the world – the principle that our belief in him must never be forced; we can believe or not as we like, but our belief, like his love, must be absolutely free.

But there was another temptation here – a test of Jesus' own faith. He'd just, at his baptism, received the assurance that he was the Son of God. Perhaps the devil was saying: "Are you really sure? Let's just try it out and make certain. After all, if you're wrong, if you've really been fooling yourself, it will be a quick end to all your doubts." But Jesus must have known that if he had had the slightest doubt about who he was and what he had to do, he would have had no right to start the journey he'd planned. He had no right to put God to the test.

So Jesus overcame these temptations to self-centredness, and he recognised that they were also temptations to rob us of three freedoms – economic freedom, political freedom and freedom of belief.

This theme of freedom must have been very much in his mind, because Luke tells us that when he returned to Galilee he went into the synagogue and read the passage from the book of the prophet Isaiah: "He has sent me to proclaim freedom for the prisoners and recovery of sight for the blind, to release the oppressed."

Jesus hadn't seen the last of temptation. In his agony on the cross he heard that same voice again: "If you are the Son of God . . . come down from the cross." Once again he refused to succumb. In the desert he refused to rob us of our freedom; on the cross he bought our freedom once for all, setting us free to serve him whose service is perfect freedom.

Non-believers stop here

For Christians, Jesus' temptations in the desert are closely linked with the Church's observance of Lent, but there's a significant difference. Both of them involve some degree of abstinence, but while Jesus had to endure temptation, for us the emphasis is more on our failures to resist temptation – on our sinfulness. But not entirely, because for the devout Christian Lent can be a time of temptation.

A lot of people quite rightly think of Lent as a time of self-discipline, self-examination, self-denial, and all these are excellent. The danger in them, and the source of the temptation, is in the word they have in common: self. Because sin is the attempt to displace God from the centre of our lives and to replace him with something else. That something may be power, or money, or sex, or alcohol, or food, or a Mercedes, or any one of a host of things. All of them are in themselves morally neutral. They can only acquire the status of sin if we involve ourselves in them in the wrong way – if we replace God with self.

So in practising self-discipline, self-examination or self-denial we must always remember that the object must be to direct attention away from ourselves and towards God, not the other way round. I think it's safe to say that all sin is ultimately self-centredness. That was recognised in the Mosaic Law. The first four of the Ten Commandments put God at the centre; the fifth directs our attention away from ourselves and towards our parents and the rest are instructions not seek our own advantage at the expense of other people.

Jesus went into the desert to plan his ministry. Perhaps we should do the same thing, especially during Lent, because ministry is, of course, another word for service. Perhaps we should spend some time planning our lives – working out in what ways we can devote our lives more effectively to the service of God and our neighbour. An essential element of that planning must be an assessment of where we are now. That means that we must take stock of ourselves, that we should stop taking our bad habits for granted but should hold them up to light and have a good look at them.

But we mustn't wallow in our sinfulness, for three reasons. Firstly, to concentrate excessively on our own sinfulness is put ourselves at the centre, which is itself sinful. Secondly, we're made in the image of God, and although we've marred that image, nothing made in God's image can be fundamentally evil. Thirdly, and most importantly, in spite of our sinfulness God still accepts us. As John said: "If we confess our sins, he is faithful and just and will forgive us our sins and purify us from all unrighteousness."

Nicodemus

John 3: 1 – 21

It's night, and a man hurries through the dark streets, the hood of his cloak pulled forward so that his face can't be seen. He stops at a doorway and knocks. When someone opens the door he asks to see the Rabbi. The Rabbi's up on the roof, enjoying the cool night breeze after the heat of the day. One of his disciples takes the stranger up to the roof and leaves him with the Rabbi. When he sees that they're alone the stranger pushes back his hood and the Rabbi recognises him. It's Nicodemus, a well-known teacher and a member of the Sanhedrin – the equivalent, I suppose, of a senior university lecturer in theology and a member of the Church's provincial synod. He introduces himself with a courteous remark, but Jesus is excited to see him.

Most of the people he meets and talks to are poorly educated and of no more than average intelligence, and he's continually being frustrated by their lack of understanding of what he's getting at. But Nicodemus is different – well-educated, able, intelligent, an expert in theology. Here, surely, is someone who will understand him. Without wasting time on meaningless courtesies Jesus plunges straight in: "I tell you the truth, no-one can enter the kingdom of God unless he is born again."

And immediately he's disappointed, because the words he used which are translated into English as "born again" could equally mean "born from above" and Nicodemus seems deliberately to misunderstand him and to assume that he's said something that's quite impossible. "How can a man be born when he is old? Surely he cannot enter a second time into his mother's womb to be born!"

And yet it's not necessary to choose one meaning or the other. The concept of being born again is essential, but the new birth has only one source. You can't accomplish it for yourself, as Nicodemus points out. How can he abandon all he's used to, all the tradition that he's inherited and built his life on, and start again from scratch? But that's what's needed. "No-one can enter the kingdom of God unless he is born of water and the Spirit." Nicodemus would recognise the reference. John the Baptist had said: "I baptise with water, but there is one to come who will baptise with the Holy Spirit and with fire." What's needed is both John's baptism of repentance and baptism in the spirit which gives new life. "Flesh gives birth to flesh, but the Spirit gives birth to spirit."

The wind plucks at Nicodemus' cloak. It's chilly, and Nicodemus wraps his cloak more closely round him. Jesus notices it, and he tries to explain again, using the wind as an illustration. The same Greek word means both wind and spirit. "You should not be surprised at my saying, 'You must be born again.' The wind blows wherever it pleases. You hear its sound, but you cannot tell where it comes from or where it is going. So it is with everyone born of the Spirit." Don't ask for credentials. Don't wait till you know the source of the wind before you set sail. It offers what you need; trust yourself to it.

But that only makes things worse for Nicodemus. He's accustomed to a strict legal code. God has given his people the Law. He's made a covenant with them and they know how they have to behave in response to it. This talk of the wind blowing freely is an attack on the whole establishment of organised religion. He says: "How can this be?" And Jesus turns on him in a combination of amazement and frustration. "You are Israel's teacher, and do you not understand these things? I tell you the truth, we speak of what we know, and we testify to what we have seen, but still you people do not accept our testimony." Nicodemus is no nearer to understanding him than the ignorant peasants who usually comprise most of his audience. What Jesus takes for granted, as will his followers, is completely beyond the ken of a devout Pharisee whose view of life is so restricted by the blinkers of legalism that he can't see that what's required of him is more than strict adherence to a code of conduct. And in exasperation Jesus says: "I have spoken to you of earthly things and you do not believe; how then will you believe if I speak of Heavenly things?" But he does go on trying to explain. Whatever our perversity and lack of understanding Jesus will never stop trying to teach us. He'll never abandon us to our foolishness. Jesus went on teaching the teacher, and what he said forms the very heart of his Gospel. "God so loved the world that he gave his one and only Son, that whoever believes in him shall not perish but have eternal life."

And we know that Jesus' perseverance won Nicodemus over. Some time later the chief priests sent the temple police to arrest Jesus. When they came back without him it was Nicodemus who said: "Does our Law permit us to pass judgment on a man unless we've first given him a hearing?" Which was just what he <u>had</u> done. And after the crucifixion the man who'd first come to Jesus by night finally came out into the open and helped Joseph of Arimathea to bury him – a courageous thing to do for a man in his position.

But he was courageous in another way, too. John wouldn't have been able to report that conversation in the dark unless Nicodemus had told him about it. And Nicodemus doesn't come out of the story very well. He's made to look inflexible, lacking in understanding, even unintelligent. But he'd been privileged to learn an important lesson, perhaps the most important in all Jesus' teaching, and what he'd learnt had to be passed on, whatever the cost to himself.

Non-believers stop here

And what about us? Are we prepared to be born again? Are we prepared to abandon if necessary our cherished customs and beliefs? – to launch out into the deep and let the wind of God, his Holy Spirit, drive us where he wants us to go? Perhaps that language is too fanciful for you. Let's come down to something more specific. It seems to me that what Jesus is asking of us is that we should be open to his teaching and ready to receive it; and that we should remember that if only we will listen he's ready to speak to each one of us individually. And he speaks to us through our careful, thinking study of his Word in the Bible and also through our prayers, provided that in our prayers we're prepared to listen to him as well as speak to him.

Putting what we believe to be his will into practice will demand courage of us as it did of Nicodemus. God grant that he will bring us out of the night of our ignorance and disbelief into the glorious light of the knowledge of him.

The Marriage at Cana

John 2: 1 - 11

One of the amazing things about John's Gospel is the amount of information and the number of allusions that he manages pack into a few words. This story is a case in point. It starts: "On the third day." That clearly refers back to what had been happening in the previous chapter, when we heard about Jesus' baptism by John at Bethany on the river Jordan, about his calling of the first disciples and about his decision to leave for Galilee. But it refers forward, too, to the end of John's story – to the resurrection on the third day.

It's about 70 miles from Bethany to Cana, so even for people who were used to doing a lot of walking it would have been three days' journey. They arrived, on the third day, to find a marriage feast in full swing. Jesus' mother was already there. It looks as if she was involved in the arrangements for the feast, judging by her concern about the wine, in fact she gave instructions to the servants. When Jesus and his disciples appeared they were immediately invited to join the party. But that involved the addition of six or seven unexpected guests and perhaps that was why they ran out of wine. When Jesus' mother drew his attention to it, he said: "My time has not yet come", meaning, I think, that his action now in the face of a domestic emergency would be only a partial, so to speak preliminary, manifestation of his glory. Contrast that with his prayer on the night before he died: "Father, the time has come. Glorify your Son."

So the scene is set. Jesus' mother says to the servants: "Do whatever he tells you" and Jesus tells them to fill the jars with water. They must already have had quite a lot of water in them, because between them they probably held 600-700 litres and it would have taken a long time to fill them from scratch.

Incidentally, I wonder if you have any mental vision of how big the jars were. They were not as big as you might expect. The jars held 100-120 litres each. A jar 50 cm in diameter and 60 cm deep would hold about 120 litres. John tells us that they were made of stone, which is perhaps another bit of shorthand on his part, because stone jars were considered not to suffer from the contamination of uncleanness, so they would not affect the ritual purity of the water.

Some people think that Jesus turned all that water into wine, and they suggest that that illustrates the extravagance of God's love, but I don't think that's right, for several reasons. Firstly, John tells us that Jesus told the servants to draw out some of the water, and the servants who drew the water knew where the wine had come from, so the implication is that it was still water when it was taken out of the jars. Secondly, it wouldn't have been a loving thing for Jesus to have done, to turn all that water into wine. The equivalent of nearly 1000 bottles of wine, rapidly turning to vinegar in six jars, would have been an acute embarrassment to the organisers of the feast, even if the guests had tried to dispose of it in a drunken orgy; especially when you remember that they had already had plenty to drink. In any case, it would have been completely out character. Jesus repeatedly tried to persuade people to keep quiet about his miracles. Such a vast quantity of wine would have drawn attention himself. It would have looked like showing off.

Non-believers stop here

It's interesting that the first of our Lord's signs that John tells us about takes place at a party. I think he had a number of reasons for that. Firstly, all the other three Gospels report Jesus as saying: "How can the guests of the bridegroom fast while he is with them?" That was a plain statement of fact. It was generally accepted that members of a wedding party were exempt from any regulations like fasting that would interfere with their enjoyment of the festivities. There are several passages in the Old Testament that use the concept of marriage to represent the relationship between God and his people Israel. John sees Jesus as the bridegroom coming for his bride. And he who is the bridegroom comes to an ordinary Jewish wedding and transforms it.

And then, John seems to see a deep symbolic significance in the changing of water into wine. Jesus had just come from his baptism. John the Baptist had baptised him and a lot of other people with water. Now Jesus showed that water, which had been used for his baptism and for the ritual purification of the guests, must be transformed into the wine that represents the joy of the marriage between God and his people. It's a foretaste of the Eucharist "This is my blood of the new covenant."

But all that's very solemn. Let's for a moment think about wine in the way that we normally think about it – quite simply as something which adds pleasure to life – something we enjoy. Wine isn't a food; it isn't essential to our existence. Properly used, it's one of the things that add enjoyment to life. So when in the Eucharist we offer the wine to God, we're offering the lighter side of our lives – our enjoyment of art and music and literature and holidays and companionship. We dedicate all these things to God and we thank him for them – the non-essentials that paradoxically are essential if we're going to live life to the full. Which is what Jesus wants us to do. He said "I have come so that they may have life, and have it to the full."

Parables

The Sower

Matthew 13: 1 – 9, Mark 4: 1 – 9, Luke 8: 4 – 8

In his version of the story of the sower, Mark gives us an example of Jesus' teaching. That's something of a rarity from Mark. In the first chapter of his Gospel he refers to Jesus preaching and teaching and he says that people were amazed by this new doctrine, but he tells us practically nothing about what Jesus actually said.

That's typical of most of Mark's Gospel. If you read it as a whole you get an impression of continuous activity, but Mark is obviously more interested in what Jesus did than in what he said. Chapter 4 is a rare exception. Mark seems to have wanted to set two scenes in parallel. In Chapter 3 we see Jesus the healer, drawing such crowds that he had to retreat to a boat to avoid being crushed.

Now we see Jesus the teacher – again in a boat, perhaps in a little bay with his audience in an arc round him. But in fact this sample of Jesus' teaching that Mark gives us can hardly be a typical example. Admittedly it consists mainly of parables, and we know that Jesus used parables a great deal, but the point of these particular parables wasn't so much to teach some new religious or ethical truth as to illustrate how Jesus' teaching as a whole was to be understood.

In Chapter 3 his works of healing had provoked opposition as well as admiration, to the extent that his opponents, by slandering the Holy Spirit, had lost all chance of repenting and being forgiven. Jesus recognises that his teaching, too, will produce varying reactions and that some people will remain deaf to his message; and Mark tries to deal with the question of why that should be so. Where healing was concerned Mark could see two reasons for opposition. Some people thought that Jesus was mad, and some that he was in league with the devil; but shouldn't everyone accept his teaching?

That's a terribly difficult question to answer, and Mark starts his discussion of it with Jesus' parable of the sower. It's a description of what would at the time have been normal farming practice. After the harvest, in about June, the farmer would probably plough his fields several times during the summer, both to break up the soil and prevent it from baking too hard and to keep the weeds down. Then after the first heavy rains – round about November – he'd sow the seed, possibly varying the quantity according to the quality of the soil, and immediately afterwards plough again to bury the seed and protect it from the birds. But in some places there might be rock close to the surface with only a thin layer of soil – too thin to be ploughed. And no matter how often the farmer had ploughed he wouldn't have been able to get rid of all the thistles, which were a perennial problem.

So this is a description of a perfectly ordinary farming process, and the people listening to Jesus would have been quite familiar with it; but it draws attention to three ways in which some seed might have been wasted. From the farmer's point of view the wastage would be negligible, but Jesus is pointing out that even when the harvest is good some wastage is inevitable. In the same way however successful his own work might appear to be, it was quite natural that there would be some wastage, some indifference, even some opposition.

That's a perfectly natural interpretation, and entirely consistent with what we believe to have been Jesus' understanding of himself and his work. But Mark seems to have looked at it from a different point of view, because although the emphasis in the parable is on the inevitable small amount of wastage in the midst of success, in the explanation it's the other way round. Now what's being explained isn't the small amount of opposition or indifference to Jesus' teaching compared with the crowds who press to hear him. Now those who accept his teaching are the minority and what has to be explained is the majority who stay outside.

At this stage in his ministry Jesus had had more success than opposition. He was more aware of crowds who wanted to see him than of enemies plotting against him. But Mark was writing for the Christians of the early Church, and for them things were very different. They formed a small minority movement in a hostile world and would be ready to welcome any explanation of that hostility.

Matthew's arrangement of his material differs from Mark's. The story of the sower is the first parable that he tells us about. He's already told us a lot about the things Jesus taught the people – notably in the Sermon on the Mount – but now Jesus introduces a new method of teaching and Matthew wants to tell us what he thinks is the reason.

He tells us that the disciples came and asked Jesus why he spoke to the people in parables. Jesus explained that the knowledge of the secrets of the kingdom of heaven had been given to the disciples but not to the people generally. He said: "Whoever has will be given more." I think he meant that anyone who had the ability to understand the meaning of a parable would be able to learn from it in a way that other people wouldn't. Matthew has Jesus quoting Isaiah: "Make the minds of these people dull, their ears deaf and their eyes blind, so that they cannot see or hear or understand. If they did they might turn to me and be healed." The trouble was, of course, that even the disciples couldn't understand what he was getting at, so he had to explain the parables to them.

Matthew says that Jesus quoted Isaiah, and there's no reason to suppose that he didn't at some time or other. Later in his ministry it would have helped to explain the opposition he was encountering. It may have been when he thanked God for having made the truth clear to his little band of followers. Perhaps what in effect he was saying was: "Apart from my few disciples no one understands the first thing about me or my work, but what else could be expected, seeing what the prophets experienced and foretold?"

But at this stage, when Jesus had more admirers than opponents, the quotation from Isaiah seems inappropriate. Matthew may have introduced it because of his own misunderstanding of the purpose of parables.

For centuries after the Evangelists' time the parables were believed to be allegories – "earthly stories with a Heavenly meaning." People tried to find a spiritual significance in every detail of the stories. And that seems to have been what Mark, followed by Matthew and Luke, tried to do. But modern scholars have questioned whether that's the right way to interpret the parables. The modern view of the parable is that it illustrates one single point – sometimes, perhaps, a few points – unlike an allegory in which every detail is significant.

And Mark seems to have misunderstood the purpose of the parables. I suppose that was really inevitable. In the very early days of the Church, before Mark had written his Gospel, Jesus' sayings must have been carefully preserved, but the circumstances in which he said them were probably forgotten; so their precise meaning and intention may have become uncertain. Mark would have been even further confused by the fact that he knew that the word for 'parable' could also mean 'riddle'. And when you remember that Mark would have been aware of the existence of Greek mystery religions in which only the initiates knew the secrets, it would hardly be surprising if he thought that Jesus used the parables to conceal the truth rather than to explain it and drive it home. Yet that can't be the right explanation. For one thing, if Jesus hadn't wanted outsiders to understand some of his teaching, all he would have had to do was to keep off the subject in public. In any case that attitude would have been quite out of keeping with the character of Jesus as we know it – the character of a man who came not to call the righteous but sinners to repentance.

Non-believers stop here

So what are we to learn from the parable of the sower? Firstly, I think we should look at it from the point of view of the sower. For the sower it's a message of encouragement. We're constantly being reminded that probably the best way for most of us to help to bring in God's kingdom is in our everyday lives – living the Christian life in an apathetic or hostile world. What we are able to do may seem insignificant and ineffective, but the parable assures us that the seed we sow will bear fruit even if we're unaware of it – even long after we've moved on.

But looking at the parable from the other point of view – the point of view of the one who receives the seed – the story reminds us to pray that God will give us eyes to see and ears to hear, so that his Word may grow in us and bring forth fruit.

But the most exciting bit of the parable comes at the very end. Seed could normally be expected to yield a 30-fold increase. In a good year, on good soil, that could go up to 60-fold. But 100-fold would be quite out of the question. But Jesus liked exaggeration. You remember the man whose friend had a speck in his eye while he had a beam in his own, or the camel passing through the eye of a needle. Exaggeration makes things stick in people's minds, but in this case it's more important than that. It's an illustration of God's generosity to those who have faith. You remember Jesus himself saying: "Give, and there will be gifts for you – a full measure, pressed down, shaken together and running over will be poured into your lap." It's all in keeping with God's incomparable generosity in giving himself to die for us. It's summed up in his own words: "I have come that you might have life – life in all its fullness."

Wheat and Weeds

Matthew 13: 24 - 30

I reckon that biblical experts are like economists. It's difficult to find any subject on which two of them agree. But I think I've found one. It seems to be generally agreed that when Matthew's Gospel gives an explanation of a parable it's based on the assumption that it's an allegory and gives the early Church's interpretation of it. In an allegory, each detail of the story really stands for something else, and you need to know the code to understand what the story-teller was getting at.

For centuries everyone understood and interpreted all Jesus' parables as allegories. It was only a little more than a hundred years ago that scholars began to realise that they had been reading into the parables meanings that Jesus had probably never intended. Nowadays all the experts agree that the majority of parables are not allegories at all. Their original meaning may have been quite different, and the people who heard Jesus telling the stories may have understood something quite different.

That's not to say that Matthew's explanation is worthless. The early Church's interpretation of the parables is just as much a part of the Bible as the parables were in their original meaning, but we need to recognise that if we can discover what Jesus was getting at when he told the story it may have other things to teach us.

The explanation at the end of the story of the wheat and the weeds is almost certainly not original. We've got to remember that the parables as we know them have a double historical setting. The original setting is, of course, Jesus' ministry. A lot of the stories are so vivid that he must have based them on an actual event. But after that all his sayings "lived", so to speak, in the early Church, and it was a good many years before they were written down. During that time they were interpreted by people who saw themselves as living in what they thought was going to be the short time between Jesus' resurrection and his second coming. Like us, they didn't know the circumstances in which Jesus told the stories, and like us they tried to work out what their significance was for themselves. It was during this time that people started to treat the parables as allegories.

One of the results is Matthew's explanation of the story of the wheat and the weeds. The experts say that there is good evidence that it is not original. It contains four expressions that, for linguistic reasons, Jesus is most unlikely to have used. In addition, these eight verses contain no fewer than 36 examples of Matthew's own linguistic characteristics. In other words the allegorical explanation almost certainly originated not from Jesus but from Matthew.

So, if the story isn't an allegory, what meaning did it have for the people who heard Jesus tell it and what lesson has it got for us?

Jesus probably told the story in response to criticism from the Pharisees, who complained that some of his followers came from the dregs of society. Why didn't he weed out those who were unworthy and make sure that the people who gathered about him were only the best and purest – righteous people? The same sorts of questions must have been asked of people in the early Church who must have found their fellow-Christians a very mixed bunch. But Jesus said: “Be patient” for two reasons. Firstly, human beings aren’t capable of carrying out the separation of the good from the bad effectively. They can’t see into other people’s hearts and inevitably there will be errors of judgment and good wheat will be rooted up with the weeds. Someone once said that the world is divided into two groups – the righteous and the unrighteous. The division is made by the righteous. That’s exactly what Jesus is warning us against.

Secondly, and more importantly, he’s saying that God has fixed the moment of separation. The seed must be allowed to ripen. The time for repentance hasn’t yet run out.

Non-believers stop here
(But I think you should carry on reading)

But that explanation as it stands leaves me feeling a little uneasy. All of us are only too well aware of our own sinfulness – aware that, as Paul puts it, our righteousness is not our own, but comes from God by faith. So if at the last day, by God’s grace, we are counted as wheat, are we to be separated from those we love who are counted as weeds? And what answer can we give to people who ask: “How can a loving Father possibly condemn anything he has created to everlasting punishment?”

I think the story of the wheat and the weeds does answer just those questions, because Jesus told the story to illustrate what the kingdom of God is like, but he also said: “The kingdom of God is within you.” And that makes all the difference. All of us are aware that we can’t possibly qualify to be considered as represented by the wheat in the story. We know that we were made in the image of God, but we’ve marred that image by our persistent sinfulness. On the other hand we know perfectly well that we are not wholly bad. In our daily lives we may do a great many bad things that we’re ashamed of, or ought to be. Our minds may often be full of evil thoughts, but we know that there have often been times when we've done good things – things that we believe will have pleased our Lord and Master. So we're not really represented by the weeds either. We're a mixture – of good and bad, wheat and weeds. And that presents us with a totally different way of looking at the story.

What I'm suggesting is that we as individuals aren't represented by the wheat or the weeds, but by the field. Each one of us is a field in which both wheat and weeds grow. That interpretation of the story accepts both goodness and sinfulness, but looks forward to the end of the age when we are judged. It looks forward to the time when, as Matthew very nearly put it: "The Son of Man will send out his angels, and they will weed out of his kingdom everything that causes sin and all that is evil in each one of you. Then the righteous part of you will shine like the sun in the kingdom of your Father."

That ties in with Jesus' teaching in the Sermon on the Mount, when he said: "If your right eye causes you to sin, gouge it out and throw it away. If your right hand causes you to sin, cut it off and throw it away. It is better for you to lose one part of your body than for your whole body to go into hell." The process of separation will be painful, and the more sinful our nature, the more that has to be cut away, the more painful it will be. But that pain won't be punishment for our sins. It will be the inevitable result of them. Everything that's dirty or diseased or distorted will be cut out and thrown away and burned. But what's left will still be recognisably us, just as a man who has had his leg amputated is still recognisably the same person. Then that cleansed, purified individual who is still recognisably us will be welcomed into the kingdom.

I think we can apply the same explanation to Jesus' story of the sheep and the goats, which I have always found quite terrifying. I'm only too well aware that if we accept the story exactly as Matthew reports it, then I will be amongst those who say: "Lord, when did we see you hungry or thirsty or a stranger or needing clothes or sick or in prison, and did not help you?" And he will reply: "I tell you the truth, whatever you did not do for one of the least of these, you did not do for me." Then I will go away to eternal punishment – my only consolation being that most of you will be coming with me.

But Paul makes the point repeatedly that if our acceptance by God depended on what we do, on our being perfect, we'd be in a hopeless situation. One of the paradoxes of Christianity is that we are at one and the same time both sinners and justified through faith.

Part of us is evil and sinful, and if we're not prepared to admit that, if we cling to our sinfulness, there's no hope for us, because nothing that is evil or sinful can enter the kingdom. But as John puts it: "If we confess our sins, he is faithful and just to forgive us our sins, and to cleanse us from all unrighteousness."

And right at the end of the story of the wheat and the weeds there's another important point. The man told his servants: "First collect the weeds and tie them in bundles to be burned." They weren't to be piled up in the field and burned in a bonfire. They were to be tied in bundles, which can only mean that they were to be carried away. Weeds that grew among the crops were a very real problem for the Jewish farmer, but they were gathered and used as fuel. You'll remember how Jesus talked about the grass, which today is, and tomorrow is thrown in the oven. So even weeds are useful. No one is so evil as to be worthless. God can use our failures as well as our successes for the advancement of his kingdom.

The Treasure and the Pearl

Matthew 13: 44 - 46

These three verses contain two similar stories about two very different people. The first was a farm labourer who discovered a treasure in one of his employer's fields. It was the sort of tremendous piece of luck which for people in Jesus' day was the equivalent of winning the lottery jackpot. Of course the odds against it were enormous, but you couldn't rule out the possibility of it happening. There weren't any banks in those days and the best way of protecting your valuables against theft was to bury them. And of course if the owner died before he was able to tell anyone where he'd buried his treasure there it stayed, waiting for a lucky finder. And that's exactly what happened at Mildenhall in Suffolk about 400 years after Jesus' time. Someone buried 34 pieces of priceless silver and they were found – 1600 years later – by a ploughman, who was an honest man and took them to his employer.

The ploughman in the story buried the treasure again and said nothing to anyone until he'd bought the field. Whether that was morally defensible isn't really relevant. Jesus told other stories about people who weren't strictly honest, simply to illustrate the point he was making.

The merchant's situation was very different. For one thing, if he was looking for fine pearls he was a wealthy man, a large-scale dealer. In Jesus' time pearls ranked with gold as being the most valuable things there were. They were thought of perhaps as we think of diamonds. So the merchant wasn't a poor man, and he didn't find the pearl by accident. He may have been lucky to be offered it at a price he could just afford, but he came across it in the course of his work as a trader.

So these two men were about as different as they could be. One was a poor employee, the other was rich and self-employed. One found his treasure by accident, the other as a result of his own efforts. What links the two is what they did when they found their treasure. They both sold everything they had so that they could buy it. They spotted the chance of a lifetime and they grabbed it.

Scholars have argued for years about what these parables mean. What lesson did Jesus intend his hearers to learn from them? What lesson can we learn from them? Some people say that the stories illustrate how the kingdom of heaven is worth any sacrifice. Jesus had encouraged his disciples to give up their jobs, their families and their security and to obey his call: "Follow me." The personal commitment demanded by the Gospel is total. All that's true, of course, but I don't think that's what these stories are intended to tell us; because nobody hearing them would believe for one moment that either the farm labourer or the merchant intended to keep their treasure. Any suggestion that they'd live in poverty gloating over it just wouldn't ring true. It's much more likely that in each case they were intending to sell at a profit. So they weren't making a sacrifice, they were paying a purchase price. And there's an essential difference between the two. When you buy you're hoping to get something of at least equivalent value to what you're paying. Sacrifice, on the other hand, is giving that expects no reward.

What links these two men is that they were both presented not with a demand for sacrifice but with an outstanding opportunity for enormous gain. What they had to do was to risk everything. And it was a risk. The labourer might have discovered when he'd bought the field that someone else had already found the treasure. The merchant might not have been able to find a buyer willing to pay what the pearl was really worth.

And we've got this same opportunity for enormous gain. For us, as for those two men, the opportunity is here and now. Here and now because Jesus said: "The kingdom of God is at hand." At hand. Not only close in time, but close enough to reach out and touch. God is here and now for us in anyone who needs help, in people who are sick or poor or in trouble.

But what's this opportunity for which any risk is worth while? And what's the risk that's involved? Someone once said that the absence of risk is a sure sign of mediocrity. We never really appreciate the things that come easily to us. The things we value most are the things we've really worked hard for and the things we've taken great risks to acquire. The husband who looks back to the day he plucked up courage to propose to the girl he loved, risking the possibility of an amused, contemptuous refusal. The mother who gives her children the freedom they need to develop their independence. The risks are high but the rewards are enormous.

You'll notice that both these parables start: "The kingdom of heaven is like . . . " And it seems to me that what Jesus is saying to us is: "Your chance of sharing in the kingdom is a piece of undeserved good fortune, the chance of a lifetime, and it's worth risking everything to get it, because what you'll gain is out of all proportion to what you pay for it."

So what's the risk that we face when we're presented with the challenge of the Gospel? Because it is a challenge. You can't be neutral about God. If you believe that there is a God, but that he has no interaction with the world, that he, so to speak, wound it up and then left it to its own devices, then God might just as well not exist at all. He has no relevance to our daily lives. If, on the other hand, you believe in a relevant God – a God who concerns himself with each one of us – he must almost by definition be the most important thing in your life.

Non-believers stop here

If you believe that God exists, that he's your creator and that he loves you, you have an obligation to respond to him. The response required of the ancient Israelites was to obey the Law – specifically the Ten Commandments. The response required of Christians is to obey our Lord's summary of the Law: "Love the Lord your God with all your heart and with all your soul and with all your mind and with all your strength and love your neighbour as yourself." How we put that into practice is something that each of us has to work out for ourselves.

It might mean taking a stand against accepted but morally dubious commercial practices, with the risk of making yourself unpopular or even of losing your job. It might mean supporting someone who's in trouble, with the risk of getting more and more deeply involved and not being able to get out of it. It's almost certain to mean making yourself vulnerable – laying yourself open to being taken advantage of.

Our Lord's call: "Follow me" is a call to leap into the dark, staking everything we have, without counting the cost, simply out of a conviction that it's what God wants. Of course we're all expected to look before we leap, but looking's no substitute for leaping so the risk's always there. And the reward – the enormous profit – comes only when we discover that in spite of all our fears and forebodings we've ended up in God's arms.

I say "ended up", but it's really only the beginning; because the way we behave as Christians isn't determined by any decision of ours to obey a set of rules laid down by Jesus. If we're to follow him the first essential is a right relationship with God, and everything else stems from that. We mustn't think of the Sermon on the Mount as being a code of ethics. It isn't. It's a guide to a right relationship with God. It's also, incidentally, a recipe – the recipe – for happiness.

But if you try to follow the Sermon on the Mount because you've got a right relationship with God you'll be taking considerable risks.

Jesus said: "I say to you who hear, Love your enemies, do good to those who hate you, bless those who curse you, pray for those who abuse you. To one who strikes you on the cheek, offer the other also, and from one who takes away your cloak do not withhold your tunic either. Give to everyone who begs from you, and from one who takes away your goods do not demand them back. And as you wish that others would do to you, do so to them."

If you do all these things, or their modern equivalents, people are going to take advantage of you. It's safer not to be too generous. But which comes first, the risk or the reward? And when you come to think of it, what better epitaph could a man have than: "People took advantage of him"?

The Good Samaritan

Luke 10: 25 - 37

Who is my neighbour? A question that I think needs to be asked, and needs answering, as much today as when the lawyer asked Jesus the same thing.

At that time it was an important question. In ancient Israel it wasn't only the people of God, the descendants of Abraham, whom the Israelites were to count as their fellow men. Heathen aliens who lived in the land were included as well. The Law is full of references to the Israelites' duty to aliens. Just one typical example: "Do not ill-treat foreigners who are living in your land. Treat them as you would a fellow-Israelite, and love them as you love yourselves. Remember that you were once foreigners in the land of Egypt." (Lev. 19: 33) It's something that today's Israeli government should perhaps be reminded of.

So the lawyer knew quite well the legal definition of a neighbour. But recently things had changed. There were far more foreigners in the land: Syrians, Greeks and especially Romans, the representatives of the occupying power. So the idea of the neighbour had been modified. Broadly speaking, a neighbour was someone belonging to the same class of society as oneself and to the same political or religious party. The Pharisees excluded all people who were ignorant of the Law and had neither the time nor the inclination to observe all its individual demands. The Essenes, who were far stricter, included as neighbours only members of their own sect.

So when the lawyer asked the Rabbi: "Who is my neighbour?" it must have been partly because he wanted to know where the Rabbi stood politically, and partly because he wanted to test Jesus' competence as an interpreter of the scriptures.

But Jesus turned the tables on him, first showing that the lawyer already knew the answer to his own question, and then compelling him to measure his own life against standards that he was prepared to use purely as a weapon in an intellectual sparring match. But there may have been more to it than that, because a lawyer would know that all that was required of him was contained very precisely in the 613 precepts of the Law; and to know what's required of you gives you a sense of security. But here was a gap that needed filling: "Who is my neighbour?"

Jesus didn't give him a direct answer. It was never his way to lay down rules. He knew how ingenious people are at wriggling through the meshes of legislation. He gave people ideals instead of rules – broad principles rather than narrow precepts. So he didn't give the lawyer a clear answer that would satisfy his mind. He told him a story that would touch his heart.

The parable has a strange affinity with a story in the 2nd Book of Chronicles. There was a civil war between Israel and

Judah. Israel inflicted a crushing defeat on Judah, killing 120,000 Judaean soldiers and taking 200,000 prisoners.

"A man named Oded, a prophet of the Lord, lived in the city of Samaria. He met the returning Israelite army with its Judaean prisoners as it was about to enter the city, and he said: 'Listen to me! These prisoners are your brothers and sisters. Let them go, or the Lord will punish you in his anger.' So then the army handed the prisoners and the loot over to the people and their leaders, and four men were appointed to provide the prisoners with clothing from the captured loot. They gave them clothes and sandals to wear, gave them enough to eat and drink, and put olive-oil on their wounds Those who were too weak to walk were put on donkeys, and all the prisoners were taken back to Judaean territory at Jericho, the city of palm-trees. Then the Israelites returned home to Samaria." The story that Jesus told would have rung bells with many of the people listening to him.

Jesus' story takes us down the road from Jerusalem to Jericho – a road through an uninhabited rocky wilderness, which even today is not completely safe. A man is attacked and robbed of everything, even his clothes. He's seriously wounded and under that blazing sun he's bound to die if he doesn't get help soon. Soon someone comes. It's a priest, going home after his turn of duty in the temple. He sees the man lying there, but the man looks dead, and of course as a priest he mustn't go near the corpse and be defiled. It's really disgraceful that this sort of thing goes on, and he starts composing a strong letter to the Jerusalem Times as he hurries away.

A Levite comes past. He sees the man lying there, but this is no place to hang about. The people who mugged this man may still be nearby, and anyway he doesn't want to be involved. He hurries on with hardly a pause.

The man's in desperate need now, but he finally hears another set of footsteps. A man comes quickly over to him, lifts him up and speaks to him. And to his astonishment he realises from the man's accent that he's a Samaritan. I think he must have been a commercial traveller. He knew the road and the inn, and the innkeeper knew him well enough to let him run up a bill.

We don't know the man's name, but his fame has gone round the world. The only name that he had in Israel was a bad name that stank in the nostrils of every Jew. But on that day he gave the name of Samaritan a new immortal glory, and it's a name that modern Samaritans must be proud to use as they continue his work of rescue and healing.

And this story has stretched the minds of Jesus' followers. It's given us a wider view of our responsibility and it's set a pattern for us to follow. But it's useful to think for a moment about how the story must have come across to the lawyer and the other people listening to Jesus.

It's essential to the point of the story that the traveller was left half dead. The priest and the Levite couldn't tell without touching him whether he was dead or alive. If he were dead they'd be defiled by touching him and wouldn't be able to carry out their sacred duties or, incidentally, collect the tithes that were due to them. That was more important to them than the chance that he might be alive and need their care. They represented the ecclesiastical authorities, but they couldn't be said to represent the good people, people who could be expected to have an especially active love of their neighbour. The priesthood was in bad repute. Someone writing at about Jesus' time described them as "idolaters, adulterers, lovers of money, proud, lawless, lascivious, abusers of children and beasts."

These men were members of a privileged profession. They represented the upper classes. So Jesus' listeners would expect the third person to be an ordinary Jewish layman. They'd expect the point of the story to be anti-clerical. So it must have been disconcerting to say the least to hear that the third arrival on the scene, who fulfilled the duty of love, was of all people a Samaritan.

The relationship between the Jews and the Samaritans was not unlike the relationship between the Protestants and the Roman Catholics in Northern Ireland. They worshipped the same God, but their customs and traditions were different and mutually intolerant. The Jews worshipped God in a temple on Mount Sion in Jerusalem. The Samaritans worshipped the same God in a temple on Mount Gerizim. They accepted the Law but not the Prophets. The antagonism between the Jews and the Samaritans dated back for hundreds of years, as the antagonism between the Protestants and Roman Catholics does in Northern Ireland. The Jews had good reason, or thought they had, to hate the Samaritans. Only about 25 years previously some Samaritans had managed to force the Passover ceremonies in the temple to be cancelled by scattering dead men's bones over the area and so defiling it.

By introducing the Samaritan Jesus excluded any definition of a neighbour that relied on a common nationality or religion. The only thing that his listeners would see that the Samaritan had in common with themselves was that he was human.

But the real surprise comes at the end of the parable. We might have expected Jesus' application of the story to have gone something like this: "The Samaritan didn't stop to ask, as you've done, 'Who is my neighbour?' He recognised his neighbour in the man who'd fallen among robbers and treated him accordingly. Go and do likewise." In other words, the point we naturally expect him to make is that one's neighbour is the man who needs one's help. But that's not the point that Jesus actually makes. Although he does finish: "Go and do likewise" he comes to it by quite a different route.

The question he asks is: "Which of these three do you think was a neighbour to the man who fell into the hands of robbers?" The point of the story is that it was the man who showed compassion, not the one who needed help, who was the neighbour. The lawyer has to recognise himself in the wounded man needing help, and the neighbour in the hated, despised foreigner who gives the help. The lawyer could recite the law of love, but he still didn't know who his neighbour was, so he didn't love him, and he didn't love God, either – the reason being that he refused to live in accordance with God's compassion but was determined to live in accordance with his own righteousness.

Jesus seems to have been trying to make him see *himself* in the wounded victim of robbery, and so the recipient of compassion, because then he'd be set free from self-righteousness – free to accept God's compassion and so to love God and his neighbour. It isn't easy to accept one's own weakness and need for help, and people who have to accept a lot of help from others often find it extremely difficult. You'll remember how Paul quoted Jesus' words: "Happiness lies more in giving than receiving."

Jesus is teaching us two quite separate things here. Firstly, and most obviously, the story tells us without any need for explanation that our neighbour is anyone who needs our help.

Non-believers stop here

But when we ask the question: "Who was neighbour to the man who fell into the hands of robbers?" we're asking: "Whom must we love who loved us first, who rescued us and gave us unstintingly everything we need?" And there's only one answer to that, isn't there? The story of the Good Samaritan is the story of Christ himself. The road is the road of life, the traveller is any human being, set upon by the bandits of selfishness and evil desires that have stripped him of his innocence and left him half dead in sin. And there he lay until a man came who was about his Father's business, a man of no reputation, despised and rejected. With eyes of compassion he saw. With hands of compassion he touched and healed. And across the centuries comes his command to his followers: "Go and do likewise."

So the Good Samaritan is a Christlike figure, because Jesus went about doing good. Nevertheless one's fellow man or woman who needs our help is in an ideal position to become our neighbour, because in *their* need they can do *us* good and be a helping neighbour to us, because the first thing they do is not to make a demand on our generosity but rather to give us something. Their gift is that in their need they set before us the real humanity of Christ, which wasn't a triumphant but a suffering humanity.

So in a profound sense it's the man who fell among thieves who's the representative of Christ. You'll remember how in the parable of the sheep and the goats the people on the king's right hand said to him: "When did we see you hungry or thirsty or naked or a stranger or sick or in prison and came to your help?" And the king answered: "I tell you, whenever you did this for one of the least important of these brothers of mine, you did for me!"

It's when I accept my own weakness, my own inadequacy, my own need of help that I'm closest to God, because in my weakness and inadequacy and need of help I represent Christ for other people – an awe-inspiring and really rather terrifying thought. But the promise is there: "Whatever you did for one of the least of these brothers of mine, you did for me."

Lost and Found

Luke 15: 1 – 32

In this chapter Luke has grouped three of Jesus' stories on the same subject. The first two describe how the average person would react when they found something of value that they'd lost. There's a spontaneous feeling of joy – joy that must be shared. Jesus draws attention to the fact that it's a normal reaction by starting the first story: "Suppose one of you . . ." and the second: "Or suppose a woman . . ." Then, having got our agreement to the point he's making, he goes on to the third story: "There was a man who had two sons . . ." Perhaps the most famous parable of all – the story of the two brothers, usually, but wrongly, called the story of the prodigal son.

The relative value of what's been lost increases from story to story. In the first story what's lost is one of a hundred; in the second it's one of ten; in the third it's not just one of two, it's both of two. And there's a difference in emphasis in the three stories. The sheep was so busy going from one patch of grass to the next that it didn't notice that it was wandering away from the flock. It was just plain negligent. The silver coin couldn't help being lost. It had no strength to resist. The prodigal son left home on purpose. His elder brother didn't even know he was lost.

Jesus starts: "Suppose one of you has a hundred sheep and loses one of them." Anyone wealthy enough to own a hundred sheep would hire a shepherd, or get a less affluent member of his extended family to look after them. The average family would own about a dozen sheep, so a number of families would get together to hire a shepherd, who would quite possibly come from one of the families and own some of the sheep himself.

So to "have a hundred sheep" can mean "to be responsible for a hundred sheep", and the whole group of families suffers if a sheep is lost. A flock of that size would never be tended by a single shepherd, so if a sheep is lost and the shepherd goes to look for it, he leaves his assistant to take the rest of the flock home. You'll notice that the shepherd leaves the ninety-nine in the open country but takes the lost one home. He has to find it, dead or alive, to prove that he hasn't sold it, so when he finds it he rejoices as he puts it over his shoulders to carry it home. It must be an extremely hot, itchy and uncomfortable business, but when you come to think of it it's the only way to move a large and uncooperative sheep. When he gets home his own joy is overtaken by a general rejoicing of the families.

But we need to remember that, as so often in Jesus' parables, these stories weren't told to his friends but to his opponents. The Pharisees had been complaining: "This man welcomes sinners and eats with them." The sorts of people who were considered to be sinners came in two groups. The first consisted of people who lived an immoral life – adulterers, prostitutes, swindlers and so on. The second included people whose occupation notoriously involved immorality or dishonesty, and who were automatically deprived of various civil rights. This group included excise men, tax collectors, donkey drivers, pedlars, tanners and, amazingly, shepherds, because they were suspected of leading their flocks on to other people's land and of pilfering the produce of the flock.

The Rabbis had difficulties over shepherds. They revered the shepherds of the Old Testament. Moses was accepted as a shepherd. David was a shepherd. God himself is thought of as a shepherd in the 23rd Psalm. But the flesh-and-blood shepherds who wandered round after sheep in the 1st century were the lowest of the low. It was unlikely that a devout Pharisee would in any circumstances become a shepherd.

Yet when, in reply to the Pharisees' accusation, Jesus started: "Suppose one of <u>you</u> . . ." he was assuming that one of them could be a shepherd. Perhaps he was trying to make them question their assumption that 'shepherd' = 'bad'; or was he introducing them to the concept of the good shepherd?

In the second story Jesus moves from the proscribed, despised shepherd to the socially inferior woman. He's again rejecting the Pharisees' attitude towards groups of people in society. Perhaps that's a lesson we should learn too. We're all in danger of unfounded prejudice against certain groups in modern society – of condemning people simply because of the colour of their skin or their religion or their nationality or because they're immigrants or because they support the wrong football team.

The woman lights a lamp, not because it's night but because the window's so small and the house is dark. She sweeps the house in the hope that the coin will either reflect the light or tinkle on the stone floor.

There are slight differences in emphasis between the two stories. The shepherd rejoices at the burden of restoration. He joyfully puts the sheep on his shoulders. Jesus is defending his welcome of sinners. The search has a price – the effort involved in looking for the sheep; but so does the restoration of the sheep to the flock – the task of carrying it home. So does the act of redemption of a sinner, supremely, of course, in Jesus' suffering and death. But his final talk to his disciples on the night before he died, as he was about to take up that burden, is full of references to joy.

The search for the lost coin is more narrowly confined, so there's the implication that the lost one <u>can</u> be found if the searcher is willing to make enough effort.

The two parables share the accent on the joy of finding what was lost, but with a slight difference. In the story of the lost sheep Jesus says: "There will be more rejoicing in heaven over one sinner who repents." In the story of the coin he says: "There is rejoicing." As so often in the Gospel, we have this intermingling of the 'already' and the 'not yet' – 'the kingdom of God is' and 'the kingdom of God will be'; 'In this world you will have trouble. But take heart! I have overcome the world.'

In the story of the two sons, the younger son realises that he's made a mess of his life, but in the first instance his motive for going home is that he's hungry. He may have come to his senses, but his senses are still self-centred and there's not much sign of repentance. He hopes that if he goes to his father and makes an abject apology, his father will give him a job that at least will enable him to earn his living. He thinks that he can earn his father's approval by his own efforts. But he reckons without his father's love. His father runs to meet him and rejoices, just as the shepherd and the woman rejoiced at finding what was lost.

But his father still has a problem. His elder son's just as self-centred as his brother. He despises his brother's wildness and profligacy, but he's got none of his brother's lightheartedness and enjoyment of life. He's been serving his father out of a joyless sense of duty. Like his brother he reckons without his father's love. Again his father takes the initiative. He goes out to his resentful son and says, in effect, what the shepherd and the woman said: "Rejoice with me, for I've found what was lost."

The story's memorable partly because at the end it leaves us wondering what happened next. Did the elder son come to his senses like his brother? Did he join in his father's rejoicing at the finding of his brother? Did he give his father the opportunity to rejoice at having found him too? We don't know. Jesus doesn't tell us.

What he was saying to the Pharisees was: "God is just as persistent as men and women in looking for what he's lost and is just as jubilant when his search is successful." It was the idea of God looking for what was lost that was new to the Pharisees.

We mustn't make the mistake of thinking of the Pharisees as completely hypocritical. They weren't. They were deeply religious people who took repentance very seriously. They believed that a truly penitent person would be accepted by God, and were quite prepared to accept a penitent person into their own fellowship. But the initiative had to come from the sinner himself. He must repent first, before he could be welcomed either by God or by his fellow men. The Pharisees wouldn't seek his company until he'd renounced his old ways.

So we can see how scandalous Jesus' attitude to sinners must have seemed to the Pharisees. He was welcoming to his table people in whom the pious Jew could see no sign of repentance. What Jesus was telling them in these stories was that their attitude to penitence was completely the wrong way round. God doesn't wait until the sinner repents. It's God who takes the initiative and goes in search of the sinner. Neither the sheep nor the coin can repent. The younger son's repentance is a self-seeking imitation of the real thing. By the end of the story the elder son still hasn't repented, in fact he still doesn't see the necessity for repentance. Repentance is a gift of God – the *consequence* of being found, not the *condition* of being found.

But there's an essential, integral connection between repentance and faith. "Repent and believe" was the keynote of Jesus' teaching in Galilee, and both repentance and faith are God's gifts, not man's achievements. Repentance means turning from sin, just as faith involves turning to God. Repentance means much more than saying you're sorry for what you've done wrong. It involves active acceptance of God's gift of faith.

Non-believers stop here

But it seems to me that the most important lesson we can learn from these three stories is simple and compelling. Most of Jesus' teaching was to groups of people, and a lot of his sayings refer to mankind as a whole or the Church as a whole:

"The Son of Man came to give his life as a ransom for many." "I, when I am lifted up from the earth, will draw all men to myself." "This is my blood of the new covenant. It is poured out for you and for all." But in these stories Jesus is talking about God's search for you as an individual – his love for you.

Our minds have difficulty in grasping or comprehending huge numbers – the fact that the nearest star is about ten million million miles away – the fact that there are about two thousand million Christians alive today. But what Jesus is saying in these stories is that to God you're as precious as if you were the only child he had.

But when you come to think of it that's just as difficult to understand as the vastness of God's love for all mankind. But we're not the first people to find it difficult to comprehend, and we're in good company. If you read Psalm 139 you'll find:

> Lord, thou hast examined me and knowest me,
> Thou knowest all, whether I sit down or rise up;
> thou hast discerned my thoughts from afar.
> Thou hast traced my journey and my resting places,
> and art familiar with all my paths.
> For there is not a word on my tongue
> but thou, Lord, knowest them all.
> Thou hast kept close guard before me and behind
> and hast spread thy hand over me.
> Such knowledge is beyond my understanding,
> so high that I cannot reach it.

But it goes on:

> Where can I escape from thy spirit?
> Where can I flee from thy presence?
> If I climb up to heaven, thou art there;
> if I make my bed in Sheol, again I find thee.
> If I take my flight to the frontiers of the morning
> or dwell at the limit of the western sea,
> even there thy hand will meet me
> and thy right hand will hold me fast.

It's a wonderful foreshadowing of Jesus' promise: "I am with you always, even to the end of the world."

The Dishonest Manager

Luke 16: 1 - 13

The story of the dishonest manager (often known as the unjust steward) has always puzzled scholars. There seems to be very little agreement amongst them about the situation that Jesus was describing or the lesson that he was trying to teach. Most of the explanations that have been put forward assume that either both the manager and the debtors were on the fiddle or that both the manager and his master were on the fiddle – charging interest on a loan, which was illegal – or that they were all on the fiddle. The only thing that the scholars seem to agree about is that this is the most difficult of all the parables.

But Dr. Kenneth Bailey who lived in the Middle East for 40 years, spent a lot of that time in Egypt and Lebanon, living with and ministering to people in isolated, primitive villages – places where social conditions hadn't altered for hundreds of years. He got to know them not as a guest or a researcher but as an ordinary resident, and he was able to find out what the parables meant to them. The question he often asked was: "If this had happened in your grandfather's time, what would it have meant?" and he constantly came up with a new way (or I suppose one should say a very ancient way) of looking at some of the parables. And one of them is the story of the dishonest manager.

The rich man starts by saying: "What's this I hear about you?" The manager doesn't know how much his employer has heard, and doesn't want to divulge any information that his master hasn't already got, so he very sensibly remains silent.

But his employer takes his silence as an admission of guilt and fires him on the spot. "You can't be manager any longer." He suspects that the manager, given the chance, will cook the books to conceal what he's been doing, or even to steal yet more; so he tells him to hand the books over immediately. But he's not quick enough.

The manager goes away and wonders what to do. He realises two important things. His master expects obedience from his servants and won't tolerate dishonesty. That's hardly surprising, but what *is* surprising is that although he's been sacked he hasn't been arrested and put in gaol. The law was quite clear, an agent was expected pay for any loss of goods that he was responsible for. But he hasn't even been scolded. His master has been unusually merciful and generous to him.

So the manager thinks up a plan that risks everything on the fact that his ex-employer *is* merciful and generous. If he fails he'll certainly go to gaol. If he succeeds he'll be a hero in the community.

The key to his plan is that nobody yet knows that he's been fired. He's got to act quickly, before the news gets out and before he has to hand over the account books.

First he summons the debtors. Only if he were still in authority would he have the right to call these relatively rich, important people to see him, and they must have been wealthy because of the size of their debt.

These debtors don't owe money to their landlord. He's not money-lender. They're tenants who have agreed to pay him a fixed amount of produce for their annual rent. The two debts represent the produce of 600-800 olive trees and 20-25 hectares of wheat, so the farms must been several times that size. In fact, the figures are so large in the context of a Palestinian village that this may be another example of Jesus exaggerating to create an effect.

The tenants naturally assume that the manager has an important message for them from the landlord, which is exactly what the manager wants them to assume.

He calls them in one by one, because he doesn't want them talking to each other, and asking too many questions. He's in too much of a hurry even for courtesies like calling the tenant "Friend" or "Sir." He says specifically to the first one: "Sit down quickly." They've got think he's still in charge. He says: "How much do you owe my master?" He's got to finish the business before the landlord finds out what he's doing, and before the tenants discover that he no longer *has* a master. He's had no legal power from the moment of his dismissal. If the debtors discover that there's any deception going on they won't co-operate. But so long as they don't know they can and will co-operate. If they know and then co-operate they'll be breaking faith with the landlord, and they'll suffer for it because he'll refuse to rent land to them in the future. There's no criticism of the tenants in the parable. They're upright citizens of the local community, on friendly terms with their landlord.

So they assume that the entire bill-changing episode is perfectly legitimate and that the landlord has authorised the change of the bills. But the whole point of the exercise is that the manager should be able to take credit for the change.

He looks at the bills and asks each debtor how much he owes. He's not asking for information; he's establishing the tenant's agreement to the amount of the debt. Then he announces a reduction of the debt – about 500 denarii in each case. The law provided for that. If trees died or a crop were blighted or a spring dried up, the landlord would be expected to reduce the rent. Usually the tenant would have to argue for a reduction. In this case a generous reduction is offered unsolicited.

Once the bills have been altered, the manager gathers them up and delivers them to his ex-employer, who's presented with a difficult problem. He knows perfectly well that celebrations will already have started in the village in praise of the most noble and generous man who ever rented land in the district.

Now he's got two options. He can go back to the tenants and explain that it was all a mistake and that the manager had already been dismissed so that his actions were null and void; in which case he'll be cursed for his stinginess. Alternatively he can keep quiet, accept the praise being showered on him and allow the manager to ride high on a wave of popular enthusiasm.

This master is a generous man. He didn't gaol the manager earlier. To be generous is one of the primary qualities of a nobleman in the East. He thinks for a moment, then turns to the manager and says: "You're a very clever fellow."

The manager knew that his master was generous and merciful. He risked everything on that. And because his master was generous and merciful and chose to pay the full price for his steward's salvation, he won.

Some people are worried that Jesus should use a dishonest man as an example, but a Middle Eastern peasant at the bottom of the economic ladder would be delighted with a story like this. Nothing would please him more than a story in which a David kills a Goliath.

Jesus' parables contain a surprising number of unsavoury characters. The unjust judge, the neighbour who doesn't want to be bothered at night, the man who pockets someone else's treasure by buying his field, the prodigal son.

But what Jesus is saying is: "If this widow got what she needed from this kind of judge; if this man got bread in the night from this neighbour, how much more will you get what you need from God? If this foolish young man was welcomed home by his father with a party, how much more will there be rejoicing in heaven when you repent? If this dishonest manager solved his problem by relying on the mercy of his master in the crisis caused by his dismissal, how much more will God help you in the crisis of the coming of his kingdom, if you put all your trust his mercy?"

God, like the manager's master, is a God of judgment and mercy. Because of his evil doing the manager faced a crisis, just as the coming of the kingdom of God presents us with a crisis. The manager's decision was to entrust everything to the unfailing mercy of his generous master, who was willing pay the price of his salvation. We're faced with a similar decision. This clever rascal was wise enough put his whole trust in the quality of mercy he'd already experienced. That trust was vindicated, and Jesus is saying that his disciples need the same kind of wisdom. But the manager is praised for his wisdom in knowing where his salvation lay, not for his dishonesty.

But verse 9 still presents a problem. "Use worldly wealth to gain friends for yourselves, so that when it is gone, you will be welcomed into eternal dwellings." What sort of comment is that on the parable of the dishonest manager?

But Dr Bailey suggests that verses 9-13 form a carefully constructed poem quite separate from the parable, and may have been spoken by Jesus on another occasion. For example, Jesus said to the rich young man who came to see him: "Sell everything you have, give to poor, and you will have treasure in heaven." It would have seemed quite logical if he'd then gone on: "Use your worldly wealth to gain friends for yourself, so that when it is gone, you will be welcomed into eternal dwellings."

Non-believers stop here

So where does all this leave us? Firstly, we can't escape judgment. We acknowledge that every week when we say in the Creed: "He will come again in glory to judge the living and the dead." God is a God of judgment. The coming of the kingdom of God presents us with a crisis. The Greek word for 'judgment' is 'crisis'. If God were only a God of judgment there'd be no hope for us. But we know that God is also a God of mercy and generosity. The landowner's generosity to his manager cost him a great deal, and God's generosity to us has cost him a great deal. He so loved the world that he gave his only begotten Son.

So we can do what the dishonest manager did – risk everything and trust in the mercy and generosity of God. That doesn't mean sitting back and relying on God to let us off the hook when it comes to the crunch – when the crisis comes. It means that like the manager we've got to take action. The action the manager took would be totally inappropriate for us, of course, but what action we *should* take is something that each of us has got to work out for ourselves. Which, of course, is easier said than done. But if, in faith, we're prepared to obey our Lord's commands, even though we can't see where it will lead us, what the result will be, but putting our full trust in him, risking everything, then we can hope that one day he'll commend us, as the dishonest manager was commended, for knowing where our salvation lies, but that unlike the manager we'll hear him say: "Well done, good and faithful servant."

The Labourers in the Vineyard

Matthew 20: 1 - 16

Between them, Jesus' parables give us an extraordinarily detailed picture of life in first century Palestine. We learn about weddings and muggings, about the life of farmers and shepherds and fishermen, about hospitality and the legal system and buried treasure and family relationships. The background to the parables is the everyday life of the people Jesus was talking to.

But he very often added a little twist to the story that caught people's attention. A man sows a field of wheat – and someone else comes along and sows weeds. A man goes to a neighbour and asks if he can borrow some bread – but in the middle of the night. A traveller's attacked and robbed – and is helped by a Samaritan, of all people. A man builds a house – but he's careless about the foundations. And, in this story, a landowner hires day labourers, but behaves very strangely when it comes to paying them.

It's vintage time – the only time in the year when unskilled labourers were needed in a vineyard. Normally the landowner would hire all the men he needed first thing in the morning, but presumably he'd miscalculated and had to go out and hire more. Perhaps towards the end of the day he realised that the weather was breaking and that he needed to get the harvest in quickly. The last people he took on may have been genuinely unable to find work earlier – there was a lot of unemployment in Palestine at the time – or possibly they were just idle layabouts who didn't want to work. We don't know. Jesus doesn't tell us.

At the end of the day the landowner was bound by law to pay the agreed wage to the men who had done a full day's work. Leviticus says 'Do not hold back the wages of a hired man overnight.' As far as the rest were concerned – the ones who had only worked for part of the day – he could either wait till they came again the next day and made up the full time, which was the usual procedure, or, if the work was finished and he wouldn't be employing them again, he'd pay a fair wage for the number of hours they'd worked.

But the landowner knew that in that case they'd have practically nothing to take home. A denarius was about a workman's average daily wage, perhaps a bit on the generous side, but the pay for an hour's work, or even for half a day, wouldn't keep a family. If a man got no more than that his children would go hungry. It was because of his pity for their poverty that the landowner allowed them to be paid a full day's wage. The parable doesn't paint a picture of a quixotic, illogical action but of the behaviour of a generous man who was compassionate and full of sympathy for the poor – sympathy both for those who were genuinely unable to find work and for what Bernard Shaw's Albert Doolittle calls 'the undeserving poor'. And that, says Jesus, is how God deals with men and women. That's what God is like.

But that's not the end of the story, because Jesus goes on to describe the reaction of the men who have worked all day. 'These men who were hired last worked only one hour, and you've made them equal to us who have borne the burden of the work and the heat of the day.' And they get the humiliating reply 'Are you envious because I'm generous?'

Part of the ingenuity of Jesus' parables is that he presented people with a situation that they were perfectly familiar with, got them to agree with a course of action which would be appropriate to that situation, and then showed how the same logic could be applied to another situation.

Jesus told the story of the labourers in the vineyard to Pharisees who condemned him for his relationship with tax collectors and prostitutes. He told it to people who considered themselves to be his enemies.

They saw Jesus as someone who was disturbing God's order. By ignoring the difference that the Law had established between the righteous and the sinner it was as if he had breached the dam that protected society against the overflowing of sin. That's what infuriated the serious, responsible and devout men that most of the scribes and

Pharisees were. So Jesus tells them a story that sketches out an alternative picture of the situation.

In the parable, too, an ordered system is violated. The men who had worked the whole day expected that the ordered, accepted system of pay would be followed. But the landowner was able to show that justice had been satisfied and that what appeared at first sight to be a breach in the ordered system of justice was in fact a demonstration of goodness. And you can't disapprove of goodness.

The immediate reaction of the people listening to Jesus would have been to take the side of the grumbling men who had worked all day, but the landowner's explanation would force them to change their minds. The parable contrasts the whole-day labourers with those who had only worked for an hour, and the scribes and Pharisees, intelligent, educated men, would see the analogy. They would recognise that it corresponded to the contrast between those like themselves who had worked all their lives for the fulfilment of the Law and the people who were open transgressors of the Law.

Jesus didn't tell the story just to extol God's mercy to the poor. If it had just been that he would have left out the second part, the indignation of the men who had worked all day. The fact that he included the second part makes it clear that he was talking to the people who criticised and opposed him. What he is saying is 'This is the way that a generous man behaves, this is the way that a loving God behaves, so this is the way that I behave. This is what God is like. If you criticise me you're criticising God.'

And that, of course, stirred up more trouble for him; because what he had done was to answer an attack on his behaviour with a parable which describes God's action. And it was this teaching that ultimately led those who could not accept it to shout: 'This man blasphemes God. Crucify him!'

Non-believers stop here

So what relevance has the story of the labourers in the vineyard for us? That's a problem that even the early Church faced. It was told originally to people who considered themselves to be Jesus' enemies. To that extent it can hardly apply to his Church or to Christians as individuals. They may continually fail him, continually let him down, but they are not his enemies.

I think we can get some clues from the first and last words of the story. Let's take the last ones first – very appropriately, as they are: 'So the last will be first, and the first will be last.' I think Matthew, like so many other people, had difficulty in working out what the significance of the parable was for the young Church, so he latched on to the fact that the last men to be employed were paid first; but that was only a story-teller's device to make sure that the first labourers were still there when the last ones were paid. Jesus did indeed say 'The last will be first, and the first will be last' on other occasions, but it's not relevant here.

So if Matthew mistook the relevance of the parable for us, what was its relevance? And here we can go back to the first words of the story 'For the kingdom of heaven is like ...' Matthew reports no less than ten occasions on which Jesus started a parable by saying 'The kingdom of heaven is like ...' And these ten parables show us differing aspects of the kingdom. It grows alongside evil in the world, like wheat amongst weeds. It grows into something big from small beginnings, like a mustard plant. It grows secretly like yeast in a lump of dough. It's worth giving up everything you have for, like the pearl that the merchant bought. And so on. And I think what Jesus is telling us here is that in the kingdom of heaven justice is important, but generosity, compassion, love – call it what you like – is paramount.

Justice is a cold virtue, and this story shows that on its own justice isn't enough. It needs to be warmed by mercy. If God were only a God of justice, if we could only look forward to getting what we deserve, we'd have no hope. But if God is a God of mercy as well as justice, that's good news indeed.

But there's a warning here, too. This story is a reminder of universality of God's love. Christians believe that God loves us, but perhaps they need to be reminded that he loves Osama bin Laden too.

But the fact that in the story the last men to be employed were given a full day's pay doesn't mean that no matter how sinful our lives are, God will forgive us anyway. Of course it doesn't, though at one time the story was used as an excuse for people to delay being baptised until just before they died so that the sins they'd committed during their lives wouldn't be counted against them. But all that's absurd because it leaves out an essential ingredient. Our response to the Gospel, the good news, must be to turn to Christ in penitence and faith. And then he doesn't just forgive us our sins and leave it at that. He doesn't pretend that we've never sinned, he counts us as righteous. And righteous doesn't just mean virtuous. It means acceptable to God. And when we are acceptable to God then God's justice is overlaid with God's goodness and love, because as Jesus himself said 'That's what the kingdom of God is like.'

Ministry

Salvation and Healing

Four of the people whom Jesus met are linked for us by the fact that he said the same thing to each of them. They are the prostitute who anointed Jesus; the Samaritan who was one of ten lepers whom Jesus healed, but was the only one to come back and say "Thank you"; the woman with a haemorrhage who touched Jesus in the middle of a crowd; and the blind Bartimaeus. To each of them Jesus said: "Your faith has made you whole."

This is one of the occasions when we'll get more out of a Bible passage if we go back to the original Greek, because the word Jesus used can mean 'heal', 'save' or 'make whole'. To the prostitute he was talking specifically about salvation; to the other three he was talking specifically about physical healing; but I'm sure he meant the same thing to all four of them: "Your faith has made you whole." And that's important, because wholeness involves spiritual as well as physical health.

This emphasis on the whole person recurs time after time in Jesus' teaching, perhaps most noticeably in his summary of the Law. "Love the Lord your God and with all your heart and with all your soul and with all your mind and with all your strength." With all your heart. You mustn't be half-hearted about it or lose heart. You must put your heart into it. You must love with all you've got, spiritually and intellectually and physically, with all your soul and mind and strength. But you'll notice that Jesus says explicitly to each of these four people not that he's made them whole but that their wholeness is the result of their own faith.

But of course this linking of healing, salvation and making whole is based on the assumption that Jesus spoke Greek. All four Gospels were written in Greek, but it's widely assumed that Jesus only spoke Aramaic. I don't think that can be right. There's no doubt at all that Greek was extensively used in Palestine at that time for both commerce and administration, and there's strong evidence to show that a large number of

Jewish families could both read and write Greek. And there are a several occasions in the Gospels on which Jesus must have spoken Greek.

When he drove the devils out of a man and into a herd of pigs the man went back to his home in Greek-speaking Decapolis, so if Jesus, a brilliant, highly intellectual, articulate teacher who lived in a bilingual area wasn't himself bilingual, then the madman, who had no need to learn Aramaic, must have been.

In the same way, the Syro-Phoenician woman, who lived in a Greek-speaking area and had no need to learn Aramaic, was able to carry on a fluent, witty conversation with Jesus.

Of course, it's very likely that even Greek-speaking Jews spoke Aramaic at home, just as, I'm sure, Gaelic and Welsh speakers who have to speak English in their work revert to their own language when they get home.

In fact Jesus was probably not so much bilingual as trilingual, because he would have studied the scriptures in Hebrew.

The Prostitute

<u>Luke 7: 36 – 50 (Matthew 26: 6 – 13, Mark 14: 3 – 9, John 12: 1 – 8)</u>

The story of the anointing of Jesus by a prostitute is told, with minor variations, in all four Gospels. It's a lovely story, though in some ways very strange to our ears. The dinner was probably a formal occasion, and when meals like that were held the doors were left open and people were free to wander in and listen to the conversation. Beggars used to come in hoping for scraps of food. So that was how the woman who lived a sinful life came to be there. At formal meals like this the Jews had picked up the Greek custom of lying on couches at a low table. I met a man recently who'd eaten a meal like that. The guests lay on cushions with their legs sticking out at an angle, like cars parked diagonally in a street. They leant against more cushions, but that meant that they all had their backs to one of their neighbours and had to talk to people over their shoulder. All just as uncomfortable as I'd always thought it must have been. The arrangement meant that the woman who'd come to anoint Jesus could reach his feet quite easily, but her tears fell on them first, so she wiped them with her hair. It must have been a great disappointment to Jesus' host.

Simon was a Pharisee and the fact that he'd invited Jesus shows that although Jesus had some harsh things to say about the Pharisees they were still prepared to have him in their company. Simon obviously thought very highly of Jesus; in fact he thought of him as a prophet. Was he, perhaps, the prophet like Moses whom the Jews had been expecting for so long – the prophet who'd deliver his people from their bondage and give them a new Law and a new covenant? And then Jesus spoilt it all by allowing the woman to touch him. If he'd been a true prophet he'd have known what sort of woman she was and would never have allowed himself to be touched by someone who was unclean.

But this wasn't the first time Jesus had been in contact with someone who was unclean. There was the leper who came to Jesus and said: "If only you will, you can make me clean." And Jesus touched him. He actually touched a leper. It was an amazing thing to do, because he not only ran the risk of contracting the disease himself, but he also made himself ritually unclean, which may be why he could no longer go openly into any town, but had to stay outside in places where nobody lived.

There's a common factor between these two incidents – when the woman touched Jesus and he touched the leper. In both cases he behaved as if they were already cleansed. In fact the same applied on the other occasion when Jesus was in contact with lepers. When the ten lepers appealed to him for help he said: "Go and show yourselves to the priest" just as if they were already healed.

So Jesus' first reaction with both the woman and the lepers, with these people who were cut off from society and from normal relationship with other people, was to restore that relationship; and when that had been done the healing and forgiveness followed. The ten lepers started to go and show themselves to the priest, and as they went they were healed. In faith they accepted the restored relationship with society, and the healing came after they had shown their faith.

Non-believers stop here

This is a living parable of God's behaviour towards us if, like the woman and the lepers, our response to his Gospel and his love is to turn to him in faith and ask to be cleansed from our sin. His reaction isn't to pretend that we haven't sinned, but to restore the relationship with himself that our sin has broken. He doesn't just forgive our sins and leave it at that. In Paul's words, he justifies us, he makes us righteous. And righteous doesn't just mean virtuous, it means acceptable to God – in a right relationship with God. The Law condemns us of sin as it condemned the prostitute and the leper, but Jesus takes the condemnation on himself, and it's his righteousness that re-establishes the relationship. And once that relationship has been re-established then the healing process can begin.

Jairus' Daughter and the Woman with a Haemorrhage

Mark 5: 21 – 43 (Matthew 9: 18 – 26, Luke 8: 40 – 56)

None of the Gospel writers really describes Jesus. They tell us about what he said and what he did, but we've got no idea what he looked like. The Evangelists didn't think that was important. All the same, they've left us quite a lot of clues about what sort of man he was, if not about his appearance. We know that he was quick-tempered, impatient with people who wouldn't use their brains. We know that he was charismatic – fun to be with. He must have been if a dozen or so young men were happy to leave their jobs and follow him round Palestine for three years. And if we look carefully we can pick up some other clues about him, too.

Mark tells two lovely stories – or really one story inside another – that tell us a number of things about Jesus and his teaching and ministry.

First there's Jairus, desperate with worry about his daughter who's at the point of death. He appeals to Jesus, and the response is immediate. Of course he'll come. But while they're on their way a woman touches Jesus' cloak. Mark tells us that she'd suffered a great deal under the care of many doctors and had spent all that she had; yet instead of getting better she grew worse. Luke – himself a doctor – leaves that bit out. The evangelists were as human as the rest of us. The woman was taking a risk by touching Jesus, because she was suffering from menorrhagia – a continuous menstruation. Apart from being physically debilitating the disease had the effect of making her ceremonially unclean. The law was rigid and explicit (Leviticus 15: 19-30 goes into great detail) and meant that she was permanently unclean and in effect ostracised. It was a serious offence for her to touch someone else, so she used the crowd to enable her to touch Jesus unobtrusively.

Again the result was immediate, but in a different way. When Jairus appealed to him Jesus made a conscious decision to go with him. When the woman touched him his part in her healing was like a reflex action. I almost said that it was involuntary, but that would imply that Jesus had to heal her whether he wanted to or not. That, of course, wasn't true. It would be more accurate to say that his love – not so much for all mankind as for each individual person – was so great that his healing power acted spontaneously. But he made it very clear that what had triggered that spontaneous reaction was the woman's faith. And he made it clear by drawing attention to her healing. If he had allowed her, when she knew that she was healed, to slip away quietly without any further contact or conversation with him, either her sense of guilt at having broken the law would have caused her unhappiness, or even a relapse, or she would have been permanently cured without realising that her healing was the result not of some magical power but of her own faith. She would have been denied the opportunity of building on that faith by following Jesus and listening to his teaching.

All this business with the woman must have taken a considerable time. One can imagine poor Jairus, already terribly worried about his daughter, wanting to take Jesus by the arm and make him hurry. His anxiety seemed to have been more than justified when they were met by some people who told him that it was too late, his daughter was dead. But it's never too late to turn to Jesus for help, provided – and Jesus makes the same point again – provided that they have faith.

Now we see Jesus in a different setting, but Mark seems anxious to link the two stories, because not only is one story inside the other, but there's another link. The woman had been ill for twelve years and the girl was twelve years old. Perhaps Mark is suggesting that the woman was able to start living again after twelve years as a social outcast, just as the child died after twelve years' life.

But whatever Mark was thinking about, previously he'd shown love in action in a crowded, probably Greek-speaking, street with people shouting and jostling each other. Now we're in a quiet, if admittedly rather crowded, room as a child wakes up to see her mother and father with three men she's never seen before standing behind a fourth man who's sitting on the side of her bed. He smiles down at her and talks to her in her family language, Aramaic, which Mark translates for us because he knows we won't understand it. And he says: "Little girl, it's time to get up." This is the man whose spontaneous healing power has been triggered this time by her parents' faith. Faith can work as well for other people as it can for ourselves. It's prayer in action.

Non-believers stop here

So Mark has shown us the Christ whose love and healing power can be found in action in a crowded street and a quiet room, in our concern for ourselves and our prayer for others – the Christ who's left us an example of love shown in the busy world – love shown to strangers – but also of love shown in the intimacy of our own home, love shown to our family and friends. But that love demands a response – the response of faith. We're all in need of healing, of salvation. We all need to be made whole. But faith is the prerequisite of wholeness – wholeness which implies health of body and spirit, not just absence of sickness. We mustn't be so humble that we become obsessed with our sinfulness. We mustn't be like the hypochondriac who's always rushing off to the doctor to get cures for ailments that he thinks he has, or preventatives for ailments that he thinks he might get, when he'd be much better off caring for his body by taking proper exercise, eating sensible food and so on.

We mustn't be spiritual hypochondriacs. We must care for our spirit as we care for our body, exercising it in care for other people, in prayer and in Bible reading; feeding it with the food that God provides in the Eucharist, all this building up the strength and depth of our faith which are essential to our health, our wholeness, our salvation.

Although all that may sound very easy, we mustn't ever forget that there are people who've been hit so hard by tragedy that faith is for them difficult or nearly impossible. But Mark tells us of another father (9: 17 – 26) whose son was epileptic and who for years had suffered the torture of seeing his son burning himself and nearly drowning. And he said to Jesus: "Have pity on us and help us if you possibly can!" "Yes," said Jesus, "if you yourself can! Everything is possible for the person who has faith." Which prompted the cry that has been repeated by desperate people all down the centuries: "I do have faith, but not enough. Help me to have more!"

Everything is possible for the person who has faith, the prerequisite of wholeness.

And when we've come to this God-given state of health, of wholeness, we mustn't forget to follow the example of the Samaritan leper who turned back praising God at the top of his voice, threw himself at Jesus' feet and thanked him.

Through the Roof

Mark 2: 1 – 12 Luke 5: 18 - 26

The story of the men who broke through the roof of a house so that they could lower a paralysed man down in front of Jesus has always puzzled me. The roof must have been substantial if it was able to carry the weight of at least five people. It would have taken quite a long time to make a hole big enough to allow them to lower a stretcher through it and they would inevitably have caused a lot of rubble to fall into the room below. In the mean time, with the possibility of part of the roof caving in, everybody would have moved outside. In any case, the owner of the house, who may well have been Jesus himself, would have objected strongly to people digging holes in his roof.

Mark says that the men dug through the roof, but Luke says that they let the stretcher down through the tiles. He was obviously thinking of a Roman house with a tiled roof, but tiles are only waterproof on a pitched roof, so I don't think his version of the story is any more likely.

I suspect that both Mark and Luke had heard that the men had climbed on to the roof and let the paralysed man down and assumed that they must have dug a hole in the roof. It's more likely that the house was built round a courtyard. The men could have stood two on each side of a corner and let the stretcher down into the courtyard itself. Even then it's worth bearing in mind that having decided to get the man to Jesus in this way the first thing they would have had to do would have been to go and get some rope.

This is one of a number of episodes in Jesus' life when we can learn something by trying to visualise what actually happened.

Both Mark and Luke refer to Jesus seeing the men's faith, so they must have seen what they did as a demonstration of their faith, even if they were not aware of his summary of the Law.

Obedience to the Law requires action, and these men were putting into action his command that they should love the Lord their God with all their heart and souls and mind and strength. With their heart, because if they hadn't been fond of the man they wouldn't have taken all that trouble. With their soul, because what they were doing demonstrated their faith in Jesus and his ability to heal their friend. With their mind because they'd worked out an ingenious way of getting the man to Jesus. And obviously with their strength , getting him up the outside stairs on to the roof and then lowering him down.

Mark tells us that when Jesus saw their faith he said to the paralysed man: “Son, you sins are forgiven”. And that’s important because it emphasises our corporate responsibility for other people and reminds us that our faith can bring people to Jesus and ensure the forgiveness of their sins. It’s proof, if it were needed, of the effectiveness of prayer.

Up till now Mark’s been telling us about Jesus’ encounter with people who had faith in him. But when he says: “Son, your sins are forgiven” immediately the atmosphere changes. Now we hear of his encounter with people who so far from having faith in him accuse him of blasphemy. They say that forgiving of sins is the prerogative of God alone and that for anyone else to claim to do it is blasphemous.

They were right on the first point and would have been right on the second in the case of any ordinary person, which of course they took Jesus to be. So far you can’t blame them for their mistake. But Jesus doesn’t leave it at that, because he offers to prove that the power that works through him is the power of God himself, and so his exercise that power isn’t blasphemous.

The way that the story is told implies that Jesus healed the man only to prove a point, but that conflicts with what we know of him. The explanation given by most commentators is that this story started life a straightforward account of the healing of a paralysed man and the forgiveness of his sins

Bartimaeus

Mark 10: 46 – 52 (Luke 18: 35 – 43)

When you were very young your body was conveniently proportioned so that if you bent your leg up at the hip your toes went straight into your mouth. I don’t suppose that that is still true for you (if it is you must be very strangely proportioned), though you may still be able to touch your toes with your legs straight. Even if you can’t, most of us can probably remember the days when we could, but I don’t suppose any of us can remember fitting our toes so neatly into our mouths.

We go through most of our lives unaware of our loss. As we get older we are aware of having lost some abilities, like the ability to run 100 metres in less than 30 seconds – or even at all – or to remember the name of the person you've just been introduced to; but there are other abilities that we've forgotten we ever had, or that we've allowed to decay because we didn't bother to exercise them, and we go through the rest of our lives without thinking about our loss.

Bartimaeus wasn't like that.

He's sitting by the road when he hears a large, excited crowd approaching. He's heard that Jesus is in town and realises that he must be coming this way. He's an intelligent, thoughtful man who knows his Bible, and from all that he's heard he's come to the conclusion that Jesus is the Messiah.

It's his one great chance, and he calls out: "Jesus! Son of David! Take pity on me." People in the crowd round him tell him to keep quiet, but he shouts even more loudly: "Son of David, take pity on me!" 'Son of David' is a title that Mark hasn't previously used in his Gospel. It doesn't mean that Bartimaeus knew anything about Jesus' ancestry. It was one of the names that were used to refer to the Messiah.

Bartimaeus knew the famous prophecy in the book of the prophet Isaiah which Jesus himself had quoted in the synagogue in Nazareth: "He has sent me to proclaim liberty to the captives and recovery of sight to the blind." Perhaps Bartimaeus thought that if he called Jesus Son of David it would attract his attention. And it did, because Jesus stopped and said: "Call him." So far, only his disciples had recognised that Jesus was the Messiah. Now a blind man had seen the same thing.

Jesus said to Bartimaeus: "What do you want me to do for you?" and Bartimaeus said something whose true meaning has got lost in most English translations of the Bible. When he spoke to Jesus he used the Aramaic word 'Rabbuni', which was a particularly respectful form of the title 'Rabbi'. It was the word that Mary Magdalene used when she met Jesus immediately after his resurrection. It tells us that Bartimaeus knew that he was speaking not just to a Rabbi or a Teacher or a

Master (most modern translations of the Bible use one or other of those terms) but to somebody quite exceptional.

And Bartimaeus said: "Rabbuni, I want to see again." The King James Version of the Bible says only: "Lord, that I might receive my sight"; the New International Version says only: "I want to see." But a number of modern translations say: "Let me see again" or "I want my sight back." It always pays to check several versions; you can learn quite a lot by comparing them. Bartimaeus hadn't always been blind. He remembered what it was like to be able to see. That's why Isaiah's prophecy was so appropriate for him: "He has sent me to proclaim recovery of sight to the blind."

And Jesus says: "Go, your faith has healed you" and immediately Bartimaeus can see again. But why did Jesus say that? "Your faith has healed you"? It may have been partly because of Bartimaeus' recognition that he was the Messiah, but I think there was another reason.

The first thing Bartimaeus did when Jesus called him was to throw off his cloak. That was the practical proof of his faith, because if he'd remained blind he would never have found his cloak again in all that crowd; and that would have been a disaster. Bartimaeus was a beggar, and his cloak would have been one of his few possessions; but he knew he was going to see again. He'd find his cloak all right. And Jesus said: "Your faith has healed you", "hath made thee whole", as the King James Version puts it. His faith had given him the spiritual vision to see that Jesus was the Messiah. Now he was to receive the physical vision that would make him a whole person.

There are two more important details at the end of this story. Up till now, only demons and his disciples had recognised that Jesus was the Messiah, and he'd forbidden them to talk about it. There's no such prohibition for Bartimaeus. The people are being prepared for the next episode of the story of Jesus – his entry into Jerusalem – when they shouted: "Blessed is the coming kingdom of our father David! Hosanna in the highest!"

The last we hear of Bartimaeus is that he followed Jesus not just "along the road", as some versions say, but "in the way" as the King James Version puts it. Remember that the first name for the Church was 'The Way'. Bartimaeus became a disciple of Jesus and one of the first members of the Church.

What an extraordinary amount of information Mark manages to pack into these seven verses! We're so used to reading the Gospels or hearing them read that we're liable to ignore the writers' remarkable abilities as writers. There's the unobtrusive ordered complexity of Matthew, the lyrical beauty of story-telling of Luke and the theological profundity of John. But Mark is outstanding for the density of his prose and the subtle allusiveness of his writing. And do you notice how he arranges his material?

The story of Bartimaeus comes at the end of a section in which Jesus has been trying to open the eyes of his disciples to the fact and meaning of his Messiahship. The section begins with the healing of another blind man, but on that occasion Jesus sent the man straight home, saying: "Don't go into the village." People weren't yet ready to hear who he was. He'd healed people because of his compassion for them, not to compel them to believe in him – he'd already decided that that would be wrong. But now he was reaching the end of his ministry – his healing of Bartimaeus is the last healing miracle that Mark reports – and it was necessary that people should know who he was while he was still with them, though even now he seems to have reluctant to make the claim for himself in public.

Non-believers stop here

But let's get back to Bartimaeus and ourselves. Bartimaeus remembered what it was like to be able to see. He knew what he'd lost. He knew his need of sight. Do we know our need? We're liable to press on with our daily lives, trying to do our own thing in our own strength, unaware of our dependence on God and each other. It's good for us to be shaken out of our rut occasionally and made to realise that we're not self-sufficient, however much we like to think we are.

We're so used to the love and support of our spouses or our families or our friends that we're liable to take them for granted. We're so used to the love of God that we take that for granted. We speak about God's love when we say the Grace together. We hear about God's love in the blessing at the end of a service. But do we think about God's love, or do we just let the words slide over us? God's love is so constant, so dependable, so much part of the background of our lives that it stays there – in the background. We ought sometimes to bring it into the foreground, to remember that we depend on it and to be thankful for it.

But there's another thing that our realisation of our dependence ought to remind us of. There are thousands of people throughout the world who, unlike most of us, would think nothing of walking two or three miles to church every Sunday, because they walk further than that every day to fetch water. And many of them – and their children – will continue to make that journey for as long as their countries' economies are crippled by the necessity to pay interest on their debts to us in the wealthier countries. Third World indebtedness is perhaps the most important problem facing the international community. It wouldn't be one of the more difficult world problems to solve if the creditor nations were committed to its solution. But we don't want to admit to our dependence on poor countries for our prosperity – for our luxuries as well as the necessities of life. We don't want to do anything that will damage our standard of living.

It's fatally easy to slip into the feeling that our own prosperity is ours by right. Unlike Bartimaeus, we don't want to see; it's more comfortable not to. We'd rather go on as we are, dependent on other people, than throw away our cloaks, come to the truth and ask for our sight back.

The Disciples

Religious artists all down the ages have a lot to answer for. As early as the 8th century – and possibly earlier for all I know – saints were being depicted with haloes. By the Middle Ages the custom was well-established, and so, apparently, was the rule that no matter what the subject matter, saints had to look very solemn. By the time we get to Victorian stained glass (if you can call Victorian stained glass art) another convention had grown up. Saints had to look old. In the chancel of the Church of St John the Evangelist in Edinburgh, for example, you can see pictures of all twelve of the apostles. They've all got haloes, they all look grim and forbidding, and nine of them have large grey beards. The other three are clean-shaven and look younger but no happier.

What an extraordinary contrast to the disciples as they must actually have been! During Jesus' ministry I suppose they must all have been in their twenties or early thirties, or possibly even in their teens. If they'd been older they would probably have been too set in their ways to drop everything and go off to follow Jesus round the country.

Think of a group of a dozen young men, living together for three years, led by a man of their own age with an unprecedented love of life. It must have been fun. They must have had a wonderful time. They must have been rather like a touring football team under the guidance of a unique team manager. No haloes, but an abundance of high spirits.

And by the time their Master set his face towards Jerusalem and the clouds started to gather, they'd found that they quite literally had nothing better to do than to follow him.

After Jesus' ascension these young men were left to go and teach all nations. And what they taught came from their own memories of those three years. I suppose nearly everything in the Gospels came originally from the memory of one or other of the disciples, so you wouldn't be surprised if the disciples themselves came out of it fairly well – if they were shown in a pretty favourable light. And that would leave us cynically doubtful of the truth of what they've told us.

We always believe the worst of everyone, don't we? In my secular line of country a screed is a layer of mortar or fine concrete spread over a floor to level it and make it smooth so that you can put down a surface finish such as vinyl tiles or a carpet. But whose fault is it if the screed starts cracking and breaking up? If you ask the manufacture of the materials that the screed's made of, he'll say: "There's nothing wrong with my product, it must have been wrongly used." If you ask the man who wrote the specification for the use of the screed, he'll say: "If the contractor had done what he was told to do, everything would have been all right." If you ask the contractor, he'll say: "We did exactly what we were told to do. It was all right when we left it, but after that the structure was bent and twisted so much that the screed was bound to crack."

In the absence of independent, unbiased evidence it's very difficult to work out what went wrong, who made a mistake, who deliberately skimped the work, who's lying. Going to have a look at the screed yourself helps, but even that gets a bit complicated when the screed in question is on an oil rig 90 miles north east of Shetland.

The funny thing is that if any of the people involved had said: "Yes, we were wrong, we made a mistake" we'd have believed them implicitly. We always believe the worst of everyone. Believing the worst of everyone is more likely to lead to the truth than believing the best of them.

Strangely enough you can apply that principle to the Gospels. During our lifetime people have questioned the Gospels more, perhaps, than ever before. How much of the Gospels is historically accurate? How much is biased? How much is myth? Provided you believe the worst of everyone you can get quite a good idea.

And what do we find? A group of the disciples being told off for trying to keep children away from Jesus. James and John wanting to use what they thought was their power in the wrong way by calling down fire from heaven on a Samaritan village, and a little later trying to steal a march on their companions by getting promoted above them. Philip not beginning to understand what Jesus was getting at. He said: "Show us the Father and that will be enough for us", and Jesus said: "Have I been with you all this time, Philip, and you still don't know me?" All of them repeatedly making Jesus angry at their failure to understand.

And Peter, the patron saint of all of us who bitterly regret what we've said when it's too late. Peter, the proof, if it were needed, that none of us is beyond hope. Peter, who at least is credited with being the first to acknowledge Jesus' divinity, but spoilt it immediately afterwards with a remark that earned the rebuke: "Get behind me, Satan." Peter, who boasted that he would go to prison and to death with Jesus. And so he did, but we don't hear about that in the Gospels. They only tell us about his denial of Christ.

And the way the whole group of disciples behaved is summed up in one short, chilling sentence: "And they all forsook him and fled."

It's a sorry tale, isn't it? We don't learn very much about the disciples from the Gospels, but what we do learn is almost all to their discredit. And this is one of the things that for me makes the whole Gospel story so credible, that these men who had every opportunity and, one might have thought, every reason for altering the balance of the story (after all, they were the leaders of the Church, and ought not the leaders to be above reproach? Ought not their behaviour to be an inspiration to those who came after them?), these men told the truth as they remembered it, no matter what the consequences for themselves.

Perhaps the disciple who comes worst out of the Gospel story – apart, of course, from Peter – is Thomas. He's mentioned several times in the Gospels, but he's really only known for two things. Firstly that he was a twin. The very name Thomas comes from the Aramaic word for a twin and John three times tells us the equivalent Greek word: Thomas called Didymus, the twin. And then, of course, there's one thing he's known even better for – his doubt. His refusal to believe in Jesus' resurrection: "Unless I see the nail marks in his hands and put my finger where the nails were, and put my hand into his side, I will not believe it."

And the interesting thing is that these two things that Thomas is well known for may be connected. Because the story of his doubt disposes of any suggestion that the man who was purported to have been raised from the dead wasn't really

Jesus, or alternatively that it wasn't Jesus who was crucified, but someone who looked like him. And that sort of accusation has been made. The Koran, for example, says: "They slew him not and they crucified him not, they had only his likeness."

But Thomas, the twin, knew only too well how easily one person can be mistaken for another. It had been happening to him all his life. Jesus might have risen from the dead, but it wasn't very likely; such a thing had never happened before, and he certainly wasn't going to take anyone else's word for it. But when he finally met his risen Lord face to face, the physical proof that he'd been demanding suddenly became unimportant.

It's interesting that Thomas received the sign that the Pharisees had demanded and had been refused, but there was a significant difference. The Pharisees didn't want to believe, and if they'd been convinced by a sign from heaven they'd have been unwilling adherents, not true disciples. Thomas' doubt, on the other hand, was based on his loyalty. After all, he was the one who'd said: "Let us also go, that we may die with him." He wanted to believe, but he couldn't bring himself to, any more, to be fair, than the other disciples had been able to at first, before they'd seen Jesus for themselves.

I think it's rather sad that Thomas isn't remembered for what he said when he met Jesus, but only for his earlier doubt. Because what he said was: "My Lord and my God", and those words form the climax of St John's Gospel. They show an insight that nobody else had previously displayed. It's the most significant confession of faith made by anyone in the Gospels. The disciples had for a long time been accustomed to calling Jesus "Lord", but Thomas was the first to confess that his Lord was also his God – to show that he'd begun to understand what Jesus had meant when he said: "Anyone who has seen me has seen the Father."

Non-believers stop here

And what about us? Our belief in Jesus must depend on what we know; and what we know of him will depend partly on what the Gospel writers have told us, partly on what we know from our own personal experience. As I say, there's nothing to beat personal experience. Every time we celebrate the Eucharist we, like Thomas, have the opportunity to touch and handle the body of Christ. But of course there's a difference, isn't there? Thomas was one of the people who were able to say what St John said at the very beginning of his Gospel: "The Word was made flesh and made his dwelling among us. We have seen his glory." But to us, and to all those who down the centuries have struggled with their own doubts, come the words of our Lord himself: "Blessed are they that have not seen, yet have believed."

The General and the Small Boy

2 Kings 5, John 6: 5 – 13

I want to think about two very different people. The first is Naaman, the subject of my favourite story in the Old Testament. Even treated simply as literature it's a magnificent piece of writing.

Naaman's a rich, powerful army commander – a friend of the king. You'd think that he had everything he needed for a comfortable, fulfilled life. But he's a leper. He's told that there's a prophet in Samaria who can heal him and after what nearly develops into a major international incident he lands up outside Elisha's front door. Elisha doesn't even come out to meet his important visitor. He just sends him a message telling him to wash seven times in the river Jordan.

Naaman's livid. "Here was I, thinking he would be sure to come out to me, and stand there and call upon the name of the Lord his God and wave his hand over the spot and cure me. Are not Abana and Pharpar, the rivers of Damascus, better than any of the waters of Israel? Couldn't I wash in them and be cleansed?" But eventually he calms down, washes in the Jordan and is healed. There isn't room here for the second half of the story, about Gehazi's greed. If you're not familiar with it – and even if you are – I do urge you to read it.

The second person I want to think about is very different. He was an unimportant small boy who became important not for his wealth or his power or his blue blood, but for what he did.

It was one day during the school holidays and he was bored and getting under his mother's feet, so she made up a picnic lunch for him and sent him off to amuse himself. He started out from the house not knowing quite what to do or where to go, but eventually he joined a group of people who were going to find a new teacher whom everyone was talking about. Obviously he was a very remarkable man; some people were even comparing him with the prophet Elijah. They had to walk quite a long way, right out into the country, but eventually they came across a huge crowd – thousands of people standing in dead silence listening to the teacher.

The boy was small and agile and he managed to worm his way right to the front of the crowd, just in time to hear the teacher tell his disciples to give the people a meal. The disciples said: "We can't possibly. We haven't any food, and we certainly haven't got enough money to buy food for all these people." There was a nasty silence, and then the boy said: "You can have my picnic if you like." Some grown-ups standing nearby laughed. Then the teacher caught the boy's eye and laughed too. He called the boy to him, took his picnic and thanked him. Then he gave thanks to God for it, broke it up and gave the pieces to the disciples to distribute to the people.

And that boy had become the person who had made the first Eucharist possible. To this day at the Eucharist the priest performs those same four actions: he takes, he gives thanks, he breaks and he gives.

So, what's the connecting link between Naaman and this anonymous small boy? Let's look at it this way. When we think of the state of the world today, with millions of people starving, millions of refugees, thousands of homeless people in Britain alone, we're liable to think: "This is dreadful, but what can I do about it?" If I were 50 years younger I might work in a refugee camp. If I were prime minister I could direct more of the country's resources to overseas aid. If I won the national lottery I could spend the money on famine relief. The prospect of the grandiose gesture is always attractive, especially if it costs nothing. But I can't do any of those things. So am I to allow feelings of guilt to destroy my enjoyment of the good things of life, of the beauty all round us, of the love and laughter of everyday living?

And then I remember Naaman's servants, who are perhaps the real heroes of that story. They went to him and said: "My father, if the prophet had told you to do some great thing, wouldn't you have done it? How much more, then, when he tells you: 'Wash, and be cleansed'?"

The grandiose gesture may be denied me, but I can still do simple, undramatic, everyday things to help. But what effect can anything I do have on world problems of such immense proportions? And there, wriggling his way through to the front of the crowd, comes a small boy with the answer. His picnic fed five thousand men.

Some people suggest that when Jesus performed his miracles he didn't do anything supernatural, he enabled natural things to happen. They suggest that at the feeding of the five thousand a lot of people had plenty of food but they all thought that no one else had, so they kept theirs hidden because they didn't want to share it; and it only took one person to make a start for everyone else to follow suit. That rings true, but whether you believe that the five thousand were fed by natural or supernatural means, the fact remains that a small boy's small offering enabled Jesus to perform a miracle.

Non-believers stop here

The small, undramatic contribution can sometimes be more valuable than a flamboyant gesture, can't it? The pensioner who puts 20p a week into the collecting bag gives more than the man who turns up once a year and ostentatiously puts in £10.

Jesus lived in a land occupied by a foreign power. He lived in daily contact with hardship and deprivation, disease and unemployment. Yet he went to parties and dinners. He enjoyed food and drink. He lived life to the full and he wanted other people to do the same, and said so. But he was always on the look out for human need and for ways of helping people who were in trouble. And it's up to us to do the same.

And there's no need for us to let feelings of guilt destroy our enjoyment of life; it would be totally wrong for us to do so. Many of us live in a world of great beauty, with enough to eat and drink and with access to music and painting, poetry and drama and to all sorts of stimulating sights and sounds; and if we don't take advantage of them and enjoy them we'll be rejecting God's gifts to us.

So let's enjoy the good things of life and thank God for them, because they're his gifts to us. But let's keep a look out for human need and for ways of helping people who are in trouble, whether they're on the other side of the world or in the same street. And then let's bring our lives and the little things we've achieved, and offer them – our small picnic loaves and fishes – to Christ in the Eucharist, and perhaps, who knows?, he'll feed the world with them.

Three or Four Foreigners

Matthew 8: 5 – 10 Luke 7: 1 – 10 Matthew 15: 21 - 28

The Gospels record three instances of Jesus healing someone at a distance, without having any physical contact with them, in response to appeals for help. The people he healed were the Roman centurion's servant, the Syro-Phoenician woman's daughter and the son of a court official.

When we meet the centurion Matthew has just finished telling us about the Sermon on the Mount. Jesus' audience would have been largely composed of peasants and fishermen, with a sprinkling of more educated people – scribes and Pharisees. Some of the scribes had perhaps come down from Jerusalem to check Jesus' orthodoxy. But there must also have been Roman soldiers there. It was extraordinarily lenient of the military government to allow gatherings of that size, but they would certainly have wanted to keep an eye on what was going on. Perhaps the centurion was there because he was on duty.

The typical Roman centurion must have come from the same mould as the modern British sergeant major – the very finest type of soldier, but not conspicuous for gentleness or sentimentality. This man had heard the teacher say more than a dozen times: "I tell you" and he recognised the note of authority. So did the crowds. Matthew tells us that they were amazed at his teaching, because he taught as one who had authority, and not as their teachers of the law.

Incidentally, the New English Bible, which can usually be relied on to miss the point given the slightest opportunity, translates this passage as: "Unlike their own teachers he taught with a note of authority." That's manifestly wrong. Who ever heard of a lawyer who didn't speak with a note of authority? It's part of their stock in trade. The important word here is the little Greek word 'kai' which usually means 'and', but can have several shades of meaning. Quite often it means 'and yet'. Jesus used the same word when he was talking about birds: "They do not sow or reap or store away in barns, and yet your Heavenly Father feeds them." So here, Jesus taught as one having authority, and yet not as their scribes, their teachers of the law. He had the scribes' authority, but the source of his authority and his doctrine were amazingly different.

That was a digression, but I think it's important, because we're dealing with real people, and if the Bible is going to come alive for us we must try to get behind the barriers of language and find people who were just like us.

The centurion was aware of having something in common with Jesus: "I also am under authority." His commands were obeyed because they had behind them the whole might of the Roman Empire. He'd heard and seen Jesus' power and recognised that it came, as his own did, from the fact that he was under authority – that his authority was derived from a higher authority.

Authority is a chain. Everyone who holds any sort of authority derives it from some source external to themselves. It may derive from election, like Members of Parliament, or from delegation, appointment to represent a group of people, or from the seizure of power by force; but they themselves can always be seen to be subject to authority of some kind. And one man who saw that very clearly was the centurion.

To be under authority involves essentially being subject to discipline. Nobody became a centurion, nobody becomes a sergeant major, without a thorough knowledge at first hand of the three elements of discipline: how to submit to the discipline of others, how to impose discipline and how to submit to self-discipline.

And this is where Christians come in, because Christians accept that they are under the authority of Christ and must obey his commandments. Most of us, at one time or another, find ourselves in a position of authority over other people (certainly all parents do) and we have to learn how to exercise that authority fairly and compassionately. We're in middle management – one link in a chain of authority, but we can't begin to perform our Christian duty as links in that chain without self-discipline – for example by regular prayer and Bible-reading.

But when we are exercising authority over other people we need to impose self-discipline – the self-discipline of humility; to admit that even we might be wrong and then to try to foresee what the effect of our actions would be on other people if we *were* wrong.

Humility was not, perhaps, the virtue demanded of the centurion. What he did display was a quite extraordinary faith – faith which Jesus hadn't seen in his own people and which enabled the centurion to see in the carpenter from Nazareth someone who had authority beyond anything his world had known.

And so when he appeals to Jesus to heal his servant he says: "I myself am a man under authority, with soldiers under me. I tell this one, 'Go,' and he goes; and that one, 'Come,' and he comes. And I say to my servant, 'Do this,' and he does it."

And I believe Jesus never forgot that man. His immediate reaction was: "I have not found anyone in Israel with such great faith." And later he took what the centurion had said and developed it into what are perhaps his three fundamental commands to those who follow him:

"**Come** to me, all you who are weary and burdened, and I will give you rest."

"All authority in heaven and on earth has been given to me. Therefore **go** and make disciples of all nations."

And to us, his servants, "**Do this** in remembrance of me."

Jesus' meeting with the Syro-Phoenician woman had an even more important and long-lasting effect. Jesus had left Galilee and gone to a village near Tyre. He found somewhere to stay and was, I think, hoping not to be recognised. I think he wanted a holiday. His ministry probably lasted for three years, so whatever his sense of urgency it would have been sensible to try to have a break at some point. He'd gone abroad for his holiday, to Gentile country, 30 or 40 miles from the Sea of Galilee, so there was a reasonable chance that nobody would know who he was.

And when the woman recognised him and started pestering him to heal her daughter he made things difficult for her. At first he didn't even answer her, and then when she went on pleading with him he said: "I was sent only to the lost sheep of Israel." She said: "Lord, help me!" and still he wouldn't. "It is not right to take the children's bread and toss it to their dogs." Which prompted her famous reply, which is still quoted in the Prayer of Humble Access in the Communion service: "But even the dogs eat the crumbs that fall from their masters' table." And Jesus said: "Woman, you have great faith! Your request is granted."

What an astonishing effect that woman's reply had! Until that moment Jesus had viewed himself and his Gospel as being for the Jews only. But suddenly all of that's changed. When he left Tyre after his holiday Jesus went back to the Sea of Galilee by a roundabout route, teaching and healing on his way, but keeping in Gentile territory. The next story that both Mark and Matthew tell us is about the feeding of the 4,000, still in Gentile territory. Now Jesus seems to have been anxious to demonstrate that the Good News was for Gentiles, too. And all because of that woman's clever, quick-witted reply when she'd apparently been rebuffed.

I think what had happened was that Jesus realised that he'd made a mistake. He'd been brought up as a Jew. The Jews were taught to see themselves as God's chosen people – a priest nation whose primary task was to bring all nations to God. So it would have seemed logical for Jesus, as a Jew, to think of his message, the Good News, as being only for Jews, leaving it to the Jews, the priest nation, to carry that news to the rest of the world. Now, I think, he suddenly realised that he'd been wrong.

Some people find it hard to accept the idea of Jesus making a mistake. But making mistakes, and having to live with the results of our mistakes, is part of being human. If Jesus had never made a mistake he wouldn't have been fully human and would have no right to say to us: "Follow me." Perhaps his choice of Judas Iscariot was another mistake.

So what we can see here is an example of Jesus' humility – humility that enabled him to learn an important lesson. We meet people occasionally who are always right. It's an unattractive attribute and doesn't win many friends. What we can learn from Jesus here is the importance of being prepared to admit it when we've been wrong. Because it's only by admitting that we're wrong that we can learn what's right. And that requires humility.

Christian humility isn't a question of saying how unworthy we are, what miserable sinners we are. That's self-centred, pseudo-humility. True humility consists of moving yourself out from the centre of your world and letting God take your place. It enables you to concentrate on the job in hand, whatever that may be, not continually comparing yourself with other people, wondering what other people may think. It frees you from the anxiety of trying to keep up with the Joneses.

The court official was probably a non-Jewish officer in the service of Herod Antipas. His appeal on behalf of his son was also met with an initial apparent refusal to help. "Unless you people see miraculous signs and wonders you will never believe." The man doesn't argue; he's desperate. "Sir, come down before my son dies." And Jesus said: "You may go. Your son will live." And the proof of the man's faith was that he turned away and started for home.

Three occasions on which Jesus had no physical contact with the people he healed; three demonstrations of exceptional faith. But those aren't the only things that these three people who came to Jesus for help had in common. For example, none of them was a Jew. They were all foreigners.

Let's look in a little more detail at the faith that they demonstrated. The fact that they came to Jesus for help at all in itself demonstrates their faith. Two of them kept on praying in the face of disappointment or even an apparent refusal to listen. The third, the centurion, emphasised the depth of his faith by his acknowledgement of Jesus' authority.

And all three accepted in faith that God's will would be done before they had proof of it. The centurion said: "Don't come to my house, only say the word and my servant will be healed." The other two accepted Jesus' assurance immediately and without question.

Non-believers stop here

We can learn a lot from these three people, and especially about our prayers. Firstly, perhaps, that our prayers don't have to be elaborate or carefully thought out. What's important is sincerity. So long as they're sincere and come from the heart, the simpler the better. The centurion said: "Only say the word and my servant will be healed." The woman said: "Lord, help me." The court official said: "Come down before my son dies." – Simple, straightforward prayers from the heart. And Jesus himself said: "In your prayers, don't go babbling on like the heathen, who imagine that the more they say the more likely they are to be heard. Your Father knows what your needs are before you ask him."

Like those three foreigners, the fact that we pray at all is a demonstration of our faith, but we've never had the opportunity of meeting Jesus during his earthly ministry, and the people we pray for have no more opportunity for physical contact with him than we have.

We're not Jews, we're foreigners. But these three foreigners have shown us that none of that matters. What matters is faith – faith that we can demonstrate by going on praying even in the face of disappointment or of God's apparent refusal to listen; faith which accepts that God's will will be done before we have proof of it.

We've all had times when our prayers seem to get us nowhere; when, no matter how hard we try they appear to be met not so much with a blank wall as with nothing, which is far worse. After all, you can push against a wall, you can hammer at it, you can patiently chip away at it. But if there seems to be nothing there what are you to do? And these three people teach us that what we must do is go on praying, no matter how unjustified or unworthy we may be.

This is a theme that Paul takes up, too. Writing to the Thessalonians he says: "Pray constantly." But he goes on: "And for all things give thanks to God." And to the Philippians he says: "In everything make your requests known to God in prayer and petition with thanksgiving."

The importance of this aspect of prayer, of thanksgiving, is illustrated, strangely enough, by someone who may be the only other foreigner for whom Jesus is recorded as having performed a miracle – the Samaritan who was the only one of the ten lepers whom Jesus had healed who came back to say thank you. And you'll remember what Jesus said to him: "Your faith has made you whole." Once again, the importance of faith.

So the example of these four foreigners helps to teach us how to pray. Three of them teach us to pray with faith and perseverance. The fourth reminds us to say thank you. And if we follow their example we may not see immediately that God's will is being done, but in faith we will receive our Lord's blessing on that fourth foreigner: "Go your way. Your faith has made you whole."

Caesarea Philippi

Matthew 16: 13 – 22

This episode could perhaps be said to be the climax of the first part of Matthew's Gospel. Up till now the story has been mainly an account of Jesus' proclamation of the kingdom of God, of the miracles which were signs of the kingdom and of the way in which Jesus taught people how to prepare themselves to enter the kingdom.

But he'd been specifically training his disciples, and although he started by asking: "Who do people say the Son of Man is?", when he asked: "Who do you say that I am?" he was trying to find out how much they'd absorbed of what he'd been trying to teach them. It was like an exam question at the end of the first part of the training course.

Simon's answer: "You are the Christ, the Son of the living God" showed that he'd learned the lesson that Jesus had been trying to teach them. He'd passed the intermediate exam. And Jesus said: "You are Peter, and on this rock I will build my church." Notice how Jesus says that he'll build his Church not on the Messiahship that Peter had confessed, not on the faith that Peter held, not on the revelation that Peter had received, but quite simply on Peter himself. In other places in the New Testament the apostles and the prophets collectively are said to be the foundation on which the household of God is built, with Christ as the cornerstone. Paul says that Christ is the only foundation of the Church, but here Jesus says that Peter is the foundation-rock. He says that he is Peter, petros, which means a stone; and on this petra, which means rock, he will build his Church.

Jesus' words are perhaps best understood as a prophecy that eventually came true. From the human point of view the existence of the Church in the early days seems to have depended almost entirely on Peter and his work. If Peter had failed there would have been no Church. But Jesus knew Peter better than he knew himself. Jesus knew that Peter wouldn't ultimately fail.

And yet almost immediately we discover how much Peter still had to learn. It had been revealed to him that Jesus was the Messiah, but now there's a sudden change. Now Part 2 of the course begins. From here on Peter and the other disciples had to learn that entry into this kingdom would cost them everything, just as it cost Jesus everything. To be the Christ is to suffer and die; to be a follower of Christ you must also lose your life.

It was a hard lesson for the disciples to learn. Their culture encouraged them to think of prosperity as a sign of God's favour. Look, for example, at the last chapter of the Book of Job, where the Lord made Job prosperous again and gave him twice as much as he'd had before: 14,000 sheep, 6,000 camels, 1,000 yoke of oxen and 1,000 donkeys, plus seven sons and three daughters. Contrast that with Jesus explaining that he must go to Jerusalem and suffer many things at the hands of the elders and the chief priests and the teachers of the law, and must be killed.

No wonder Peter couldn't accept it. Yet no wonder Jesus was angry with him. It's all too easy to forget that Jesus was human, as human as you or me. He'd come to realise that his decision to do what he believed he had to do was bound to lead to his being arrested and executed. It must have taken tremendous courage to make that decision in cold blood.

Now here was Peter trying to weaken his resolve, suggesting that Jesus could fulfil his destiny by establishing himself as the kind of Messiah that the Jews had come to expect – a leader who would drive out the Romans and restore the sort of kingdom that David had ruled over.

This beginning of the second part of Jesus' ministry is remarkably like the beginning of the first part. The first time we hear of Jesus as an adult is when he comes to the Jordan to be baptised by John and he hears a voice from heaven saying: "This is my Son." That's followed immediately by Jesus' temptation in the wilderness, with the devil showing him all the kingdoms of the world and their splendour, and saying: "All this I will give you if you will bow down and worship me."

The second part of his ministry begins with Peter saying: "You are the Son of God." That's followed immediately by Peter repeating that same temptation to world dominance. No wonder Jesus said: "Get behind me, Satan." He must have recognised Peter's words as the voice of the devil, and perhaps what he was saying was: "I've already put this behind me and I'm not going to listen."

This isn't the first time Peter's recorded as making a fool of himself, and it won't be the last. But Jesus knew that beneath the weak, shifting sand that could be swept away by the first storm and was no use for building anything on, lay the solid rock on which he could build his Church. So he kept on training Peter, even though at times it must have seemed a hopeless task; and only six days after the conversation at Caesarea Philippi Jesus took Peter, with James and John, up a high mountain by themselves and allowed them to see him transfigured.

The transfiguration confirmed the revelation to Peter that Jesus was the Son of God, but it also confirmed the imminence of his death. It was a continuation of the second phase of the disciples' training. But the fact that he was allowed to witness the transfiguration was also a reassurance to Peter that although he'd started this second phase badly Jesus hadn't given up on him. And when things got worse, when Peter and the other disciples forsook him and fled, when Peter denied all knowledge of him, when it looked as if he'd utterly failed, Jesus still didn't give up on Peter. And the last time we see them together Jesus gives Peter a job to do: "Feed my sheep" and his last recorded words are: "Follow me."

Non-believers stop here

And what about us? The first part of our training course isn't too difficult. We can accept without difficulty our Lord's proclamation of the kingdom of God. We can accept his teaching about how we are to prepare ourselves to enter the kingdom. We can join Peter in saying: "You are the Christ, the Son of the living God." We can pass the exam at the end of the first part of the training course. But none of that requires any great commitment.

Like Peter, we've got to learn that to be the Christ is to suffer and die, and be a follower of Christ is also to lose one's life. Jesus said to his disciples, and he says to us, because we're his disciples, too: "If anyone would come after me, he must deny himself and take up his cross and follow me. For whoever wants to save his life will lose it, but whoever loses his life for me will find it." When Jesus said: "He must deny himself" he used the same word that he used when he told Peter that he would deny him three times, that he would dissociate himself from Jesus. Self-denial means dissociation from self.

That's perhaps the hardest part of the Gospel for us to learn, especially as we live in a society that gives such emphasis to the importance of success and the acquisition of wealth.

It requires a level of commitment that we find it very difficult to maintain. Part 2 of the course is far more demanding than Part 1. We're only too well aware that we'll persistently fail to meet its demands, just as Peter did, but as Paul said: "Nothing can separate us from the love of God in Christ Jesus" and just as Jesus never gave up on Peter, he'll never give up on us, either.

Transfiguration

Matthew 17: 1 – 8 Mark 9: 2 – 8 Luke 9: 28 - 36

Anyone who sets out to write a life of Christ, a biography of Jesus (which this is not), must run into difficulties very quickly, because the people who wrote the Gospels weren't primarily concerned with historical accuracy and completeness; so that there are discrepancies between the four Gospels and all of them leave tantalising gaps. The reason is, of course, that the evangelists' chief concern was to record the truth as they perceived it; and so the Gospels are rather like a series of impressionist paintings, not a series of photographs.

A painting by one of the great impressionists can convey something of the atmosphere of a scene that might well be completely missing from a photograph of the same place. And in the same way, an evangelist's description of an episode in the life of Jesus may well convey more of the truth than an accurate historical report. But in some cases the evangelists had to try to report occurrences that were so far outside everyday human experience that there were no words to describe them.

If you made friends with a primitive tribesman, perhaps from the upper Amazon, and took him to see a Formula 1 Grand Prix, and then took him home and asked him to describe his experience to his friends, he'd find himself almost completely unable to do so. He could describe the noise and the smells and the colours and the sense of movement, but he might well have failed to understand the significance of what he'd seen; and even if he had understood it he wouldn't have the words to describe it. All that he could do would be to describe the impression it had made on him.

And that, it seems to me, is what's happened over some of the incidents in the Bible. The people who witnessed them had no words to describe what they'd experienced. Some of these stories may be myths conveying important truths but not based on historical fact, as I suggested when discussing the stories surrounding the account of Jesus' birth, but I don't think that's necessarily always true. When Van Gogh painted a cornfield it was a painting of an actual cornfield, even though a photograph of the same scene would have looked quite different.

And one of the most outstanding examples of an episode that the witnesses had no words to describe was Jesus' transfiguration. They had no words to describe it, but it's interesting to look at the words they did use and to see the significance that it had for them.

Mark's account, for example, starts: "After six days." This is the only occasion in the whole of his Gospel on which Mark is so specific about a time, so it must have been significant for him. He doesn't say what it was six days after, but he's just been describing the episode at Caesarea Philippi when Peter confessed his faith that Jesus was the Messiah and when Jesus warned the disciples of the necessity of his suffering and death; and by saying: "After six days" Mark is linking the stories of Caesarea Philippi and the transfiguration.

Perhaps he saw them as two episodes of a single experience. Perhaps Jesus chose only Peter, James and John to witness his transfiguration because only James and John shared the insight demonstrated by Peter's confession. Jesus was always careful not to compel people to believe in him, so the experience of his three friends at his transfiguration came as a confirmation of their faith rather than a cause of it. That could well be the reason why he told them not to talk about what they'd seen 'until the Son of Man had risen from the dead'. By that time a wider group had come to share the insight of the first three, and their faith was confirmed rather than caused by what the three told them.

The period of six days may have had another significance for Mark. It's possible that it was traditionally the length of time required for preparation and self-purification before a close approach to God. Or it may be the first of several references back to the Old Testament. The book Exodus tells us: "For six days the cloud covered the mountain, and on the seventh day the Lord called to Moses from within the cloud" (24: 16). Perhaps Mark is saying that now, on the seventh day, God called to the new Moses from within the cloud.

When Moses came down from Sinai, the skin of his face shone because he had spoken with God. Mark stresses the whiteness of Jesus' garments and says that when he came down from the mountain the crowd of people who ran to meet him were greatly amazed. Luke adds that the appearance of his face changed. So I think it's obvious that the evangelists want us to compare the transfiguration with Moses' meeting with God on Mount Sinai.

The Mount of the Transfiguration is the new Sinai. There's no point in trying to identify it geographically because the evangelists had no more interest in geography for its own sake than they had in history.

The disciples saw Moses and Elijah with Jesus – representing the Law and the prophets – both of them bearing testimony to Jesus; but their appearance is also a reference back to Malachi: "Remember the law of my servant Moses, the decrees and laws I gave him at Horeb for all Israel. See, I will send you the prophet Elijah before that great and dreadful day of the Lord comes" (4: 4-5).

Peter's suggestion that they should build three tabernacles isn't the naïve remark that it seems to be at first sight. It's an essential part of the symbolism of the story. The Jews had come to look forward to the Messiah tabernacling with his righteous chosen ones. Ezekiel wrote: "My dwelling-place will be with them; I will be their God, and they will be my people." (37: 27). The theme of God dwelling among his people runs through the later books of the Old Testament and there are half a dozen references to God dwelling in a tent.

Perhaps Peter wanted to make permanent a vision that could only be temporary. But what he failed to realise was that this wasn't the final appearance of Christ in his glory but only a foreshadowing of it. Jesus still had to suffer and die and overcome death.

And then the cloud comes down – the cloud that had been a sign of God's presence, the Shekinah, in the story of the Exodus – and they hear a voice saying the same thing that was said at Jesus' baptism in the river Jordan: "This is my Son, whom I love." But then there's a significant addition: "Listen to him!", which is another quotation, this time from Deuteronomy, in which Moses says: "The Lord your God will raise up for you a prophet like me from among your own brothers. You must listen to him" (18: 15). And after the disciples have heard the voice they find that the cloud has gone and Moses and Elijah have vanished. They represent the old order, which has been fulfilled.

So the transfiguration confirmed the disciples' perception of Jesus as the Messiah. But the voice they heard also confirmed that Jesus' teaching that he must suffer was in accordance with the will of God.

It's worth noticing that the transfiguration took place for the benefit of the three disciples. Mark says: "He was transfigured before *them*." "There appeared before *them* Elijah and Moses." "A cloud appeared and enveloped *them*." The voice said: "*Listen* to him." "Suddenly, when they looked round, they no longer saw anyone with *them* except Jesus."

Non-believers stop here

So what relevance has all this for us? I suppose firstly and very simply that the evangelists were writing for people who knew their Bibles. The average Jew of the first century, and even probably many of the Gentile early Christians, had a much better knowledge of what we know as the Old Testament than most of us do. And as they read this story, or heard it read on Sundays, they would have recognised the references and understood what the writer was trying to convey. So if this story does nothing else it warns us that we're liable to fail to understand some of the message of the Gospels unless we study the Old Testament as well as the New.

But, more importantly, the transfiguration was, for the men who witnessed it, a means of reassurance about the things that all Christians hope for. There were grim times ahead – for Jesus at his trial and crucifixion, for the disciples after his resurrection, for Christians all down the ages suffering persecution and ridicule and personal tragedy; but to Peter and James and John, and to all who are prepared to believe their testimony, the transfiguration is a sign that the faith and hope of the Gospel of Christ are not an illusion.

I said just now that the transfiguration took place for the benefit of the three disciples. But if it was for their benefit it was for ours, too. Jesus said to the two disciples on their way to Emmaus: "Did not Christ have to suffer these things and then enter his glory?" And in the transfiguration God gave the disciples – and us – evidence that although the glory had to be preceded by the suffering, yet just as surely the suffering would be followed by the glory.

It's that glory that we acknowledge and look forward to every time we say the Lord's Prayer. We've said it so often that we're liable not even to notice what we're saying: "Thine is the kingdom, the power and the glory."

Peter himself sums it all up in his second Epistle: "We were eye-witnesses of his majesty. For he received honour and glory from God the Father when the voice came to him from the Majestic Glory, saying, 'This is my Son, whom I love; with him I am well pleased.' We ourselves heard this voice that came from heaven when we were with him on the sacred mountain."

Eternal Life

Matthew 19: 16-29

In this book I've been looking at passages of scripture and exploring their relevance to us as we lead our daily lives. It's not always easy to find something to say that I hope you'll find interesting, or to draw conclusions from it that aren't trite or pious platitudes. But I haven't so far come across anything quite as difficult as Jesus' conversation with the rich young man. "Go, sell your possessions and give to the poor, and you will have treasure in heaven. Then come, follow me." Did Jesus really mean that that's what we're all to do? Does he really require me to urge you to sell all your possessions and give to the poor? And if not, what does he require of us?

Let's go back to the beginning. The young man had said: "Teacher, what good thing must I do to get eternal life?" That was a standard question to which in Jesus' time there was a generally accepted answer. You had to build up a credit balance of virtue for yourself. You'd be judged by your good deeds. And the Jews were generally agreed on how you ought to go about it. God's will for man had been revealed in the Law of Moses, and those who kept that law would automatically qualify.

The trouble was that the scribes and Pharisees had extended the law with so many minute, detailed requirements that only the rich had any hope of qualifying. Anyone who had to work for his living simply didn't have the time. But Jesus ignores all the additional stuff and simply quotes five of the Ten Commandments plus the passage from Leviticus: "Love your neighbour as yourself."

But the young man says: "I've kept all these. Where do I still fall short?" That wasn't boastfulness. A devout Jew treasured his consciousness of living by the Law. Jesus' reply contains the essence of all St Paul's later teaching about the Law. Keeping the Law isn't enough. You're justified not by works but by faith – by relying entirely on God's mercy.

But that's exactly what the young man couldn't do. It's terribly difficult for very wealthy people to give up their wealth, because it means depriving themselves of the very resources that they've come to rely on for status and security. No wonder the disciples were amazed when Jesus said how hard a rich man would find it to enter the kingdom of heaven. They'd been brought up to believe that worldly wealth was a sign of God's favour.

After the young man had gone sadly away, Peter said: "We have left everything to follow you! What then will there be for us?" And Jesus answered: "Everyone who has left houses or brothers or sisters or father or mother or children or fields for my sake will receive a hundred times as much and will inherit eternal life." Does Jesus really want us not only to give up our possessions but to abandon our families? The outrageousness of any suggestion that Jesus was saying that it's right to abandon our children seems in a way to be helpful because it forces us to look behind Matthew's stark narrative and try to work out what Jesus was really getting at in both these conversations.

There are two things that we must bear in mind. Firstly, Jesus, like other teachers who've made the deepest impression on people's imagination, loved to present his ideas in extreme form. Probably no English writer in the nineteenth century had more influence than Charles Dickens. His pictures of the misery of the poor opened people's eyes to what was going on and hastened many of our social reforms, while on a lighter side he's had a lasting effect on our Christmas festivities. But all his most famous characters were extremes – caricatures drawn without any regard to the circumstances of daily life. But that was what caught people's imagination. And, of course, still does.

And Jesus, another master story-teller, used the same technique to catch people's imagination. He put things in an extreme way and startled people with paradoxes. He caught their attention and made them think. "If your right hand is your undoing, cut it off and throw it away." "Why do you look at the speck of dust in your brother's eye with never a thought for the great plank in your own?"

It's not safe to take one of Jesus' utterances out of context and treat it as a literal rule of conduct for all Christians for all time. He himself who said: "Offer the wicked man no resistance" whipped the money-changers out of the temple. And it's also true that he didn't command or even allow everyone to leave home and follow him. Do you remember the man whose legion of devils had gone into the Gadarene swine? Afterwards the man begged to go with him, but Jesus wouldn't allow it, and said: "Go home to your own folk and tell them what the Lord in his mercy has done for you."

But in spite of that, Jesus does demand from his disciples submission to wrong and injustice as far as their own pride and self-interest are concerned, and right from the beginning he did detach from their homes and businesses the men he intended to train as his agents.

And that brings us to the second thing that we must bear in mind. His time was short. He probably foresaw that he wouldn't be allowed to live long, that he was likely to die having appeared to fail. But he was preparing for a greater future. He was training the people to whom the Gospel could be entrusted after he'd gone, and these people must be detached from earthly ties. They must be ready, physically as well as spiritually, to follow the Son of Man who had nowhere to lay his head.

We can detect this feeling of urgency in the instructions that Jesus gave to his disciples when he sent them out to preach the kingdom of God and to heal the sick: "Take nothing for the journey – no staff, no bag, no bread, no money, no extra tunic." There was no time to be lost. They mustn't be burdened with surplus equipment. They mustn't waste their time with people who were unreceptive. This was the sort of work they were going to have to do if they were to spread the Gospel after his ascension. Perhaps he wanted to give them practical experience while he was still able to discuss their successes and failures with them.

It's this preparation for the future by training his disciples that more and more appears to be in Jesus' mind, and it explains a lot in what he said that we find difficult. At the last moment it looked as if he'd failed. His chosen instrument seemed to break in his hand. Even the twelve couldn't stand the strain. But at his ascension he left behind what he'd wanted – a body of men who were bound by no earthly ties, who had no concern with property, who made no demand for pleasure – a body capable of anything.

So if we're to understand these hard sayings we must understand that what we're shown in the Gospels is a preparation for the future. The Gospels contain an ideal, stated in its most startling form; and they describe the training of a small body of men who had to work out that ideal.

But the Gospels don't stand alone. They're bound up with the records of the early Church in the Acts of the Apostles and the Epistles. The Gospels were written later than many of the Epistles and are a record of what the Church remembered of its great beginning.

And in the Acts of the Apostles and the Epistles we find a society which believes in the kingdom of God as having already come, but which is outwardly living the normal life of the rest of the community – the life of husbands and wives, parents and children, masters and servants – a society which assumes that this normal human life is no contradiction of the Lord's teaching.

So we find in the Gospels both what concerns the enduring nature of the kingdom of God and what belongs especially to the time of preparation – of the training – of the disciples. I think we can say that the conversations we've been considering belong to the training period. They were spoken to the Twelve, and Jesus did demand those sacrifices of them.

Non-believers stop here

But although in this startling form these words aren't a literal rule of conduct for us, yet we must recognise that behind them is teaching that concerns the enduring nature of the kingdom of God – teaching that is binding on all Christians at all times; teaching that sacrifice is an essential part of Christianity. We can't be followers of Christ without sacrifice. How great that sacrifice must be is something that each one of us must work out for ourselves. We may not feel that "Sell your possessions and give to the poor" is a literal instruction that we must obey. We may not believe that Jesus requires us to abandon our families; but his words do warn us not to cling to tightly to material things; not to become like the rich young man, so reliant on our possessions that they become our master. His words require us to ask ourselves: "What is my Christianity costing me? Am I too dependent on material things? And, above all, do I really try to obey Jesus' command, which certainly is for each one of us, for all time: 'Seek first the kingdom of God'?"

Render to Caesar

Matthew 22: 16 – 21, Mark 12: 14 – 17, Luke 20: 21 – 25

One of the remarkable things about the Gospels is that in so many cases we can see an immediate relevance to our lives of the stories they tell. We can identify with the people who came to Jesus – people who were hungry or frightened or ill or sad. We can see the relevance of his stories to our condition even though they were told to people whose culture was very different from ours. But there are occasions when we can miss a great deal if we don't know the background and the context of an event or a conversation. And this discussion about payment of taxes to Caesar is one of them. All the way through it's packed with meaning that would have been obvious to a contemporary Jew but is far from obvious to us. Let's look at it in a bit more detail

The Pharisees get together with the Herodians and hatch up a catch question for Jesus. They make a strange alliance. The Pharisees resented the Romans. The Herodians were pro-Roman collaborators because it was the Roman army that had put Herod on the throne. But they agreed on the ingenuity of the question: "Is it lawful to pay tribute to Caesar?" If Jesus said: "No" the Herodians would denounce him to the Roman governor as a subversive agitator. If he said: "Yes" he'd alienate himself from the majority of people who bitterly resented the Roman taxes.

Economically, the Jews were in a dreadful state. They were in a unique position. Other nations paid taxes largely to support a standing army, as most nations still do. When they were defeated by Rome those taxes ceased and were replaced by taxes paid to Rome. But the Jews never had a standing army. They considered themselves to be under the rule and protection of God, and their taxes went towards the maintenance of the temple and its priests. These taxes didn't cease when the country was conquered by Rome. So the Jews found themselves in an impossible position. The Roman attitude was: "You're living within the Roman Empire; you enjoy all its benefits. Make what financial arrangements you like with your religious leaders, but it goes without saying that you must pay your taxes to Rome." And the attitude of the priests was: "If you manage to avoid paying your taxes to Rome we'll regard you as a patriot rather than a sinner, but not to pay your religious dues would be blasphemous. You'd be robbing God, not man."

So the question: "Is it lawful to pay tribute to Caesar?" was a very awkward one, and it's characteristic of Jesus that he should ask them a question in reply: "Why do you set this trap for me?" But he goes on: "Let me see the money you pay the tax with." The tax had to be paid with a silver denarius; the copper coins minted in Palestine for everyday use wouldn't do. The silver coins were hated by everyone. They were a symbol of the Jews' subjection to Rome. They had Caesar's head on them, so they were loathed by the extreme nationalists; and the inscription referred to Caesar as a god, so they were loathed by the devout religious people.

But Jesus asked his questioners to produce one of these hated coins. The fact that they possessed one showed that they used the emperor's coinage and accepted what it symbolised. Jesus asked them to identify the image on it, and then he pointed out that these coins belonged to Caesar. They were used as pay for the Roman army, and that meant that the people who used them acknowledged the authority of Rome and accepted the benefits of Roman rule that were symbolised by the coin.

Then comes that famous instruction – one of the best-known sayings in the Bible: "Render unto Caesar the things that are Caesar's and unto God the things that are God's." But the word translated as "Render" in the Authorised Version isn't the same as the word in the original question: "Is it lawful to pay tribute to Caesar?" Modern translations of the Bible vary in the words they use, but the Jerusalem Bible has it right: "Give back to Caesar what belongs to Caesar – and to God what belongs to God."

It was generally accepted in Jesus' time that coins issued in the name of a ruler and with his insignia on them were the personal property of the ruler. So the payment of the silver coins to Caesar was the payment of a debt. In effect, what Jesus was saying was: "You owe a debt to Caesar for the benefits that you receive from being part of the Roman empire, and that debt must be paid. And you owe a debt to God for all the benefits that you receive from his love, and that debt must be paid too."

That doesn't, of course, mean that the secular and the sacred belong in two independent, separate compartments. It means that men and women are subjects of two kingdoms – one earthly and one Heavenly – and owe a debt of loyalty to both of them. But there's a difference, because God deals with mankind partly through the impersonal and fallible institutions of society and civil government and partly through the direct and personal impact of his love.

So long as Caesar performs his God-given function of providing a framework of law and order for everyday life he has a right to claim what is due to him. The payment of taxes is a moral obligation. It's a different matter if Caesar starts claiming absolute and unconditional obedience, because that belongs by right only to God. For a ruler to make that sort of claim is totalitarianism.

But we've got to be careful, because the same thing happens if religion tries to take over the functions of the state. The Zealots of Jesus' time believed that allegiance to Caesar was disloyalty to God and that the only course open to the people of God was to regain their independence by force and establish a theocracy. But all theocracy is by nature totalitarian, because it confuses human institutions with divine ordinances. To impose a human law on people on the grounds that it's the will of God is to leave the people with no freedom of choice, no free will.

Non-believers stop here

So where does that leave us? Our situation is very different from that of the Jews of Jesus' time. We live in a democracy, we're not ruled by a foreign power, we don't suffer from double taxation, though it sometimes feels like it. But Jesus' words do apply to us all the same, because just as we must pay our debt to Caesar, so we must pay our debt to God. We've received his love, freely given, unearned and undeserved; and what he requires of us is our love in return. And paradoxically we can show our love for him best by our love and care for other people, by being the channels of his love for them.

Zacchaeus

Luke 19: 1 - 10

Although there's a certain amount of humour in the Gospels, we don't really expect to find any comic relief. I think the nearest we get to it is in that story about Zacchaeus. I think of him as being small, dapper and overweight. A man who has spent most of his working life at an office desk. A tax collector.

The Roman authorities saved themselves the trouble and expense of collecting taxes by selling the contract for collection to a syndicate of businessmen in Rome. They in turn employed agents who were paid by commission. They got a rake-off from all the taxes they could screw out of people, and there was very little they didn't tax. Tax collectors were especially hated by strict Jews, who considered them to be ceremonially unclean, because of their continual contact with Gentiles and their need to work on the Sabbath. Zacchaeus was a chief tax-collector — certainly rich, but not popular.

But though he had worked for Rome for most of his life he was still a Jew, and he knew the Law – the Law that said 'Love God and your neighbour'. People didn't, of course. He reckoned that a man had only so much love in him. Enough for himself and maybe his wife and kids. Perhaps even a bit to spare for a couple of close friends, but no more than that. It wasn't that he didn't want to love his neighbour; he just didn't dare let himself. He hadn't enough love to go round. After all, charity began at home, didn't it? And ended there.

Then someone told him that Jesus was coming to town. He'd heard about this man. One of Zacchaeus's colleagues was a man called Levi. He didn't know him well, though they used to meet occasionally at tax-collectors' conferences. But he'd met Levi a few weeks ago and he was like a different man. He'd left the revenue service and changed his name to Matthew, simply in order to follow a carpenter from Nazareth. Now he radiated happiness in a way that Zacchaeus had never seen before.

So when he heard that Jesus was coming through Jericho, Zacchaeus thought he must go and see what he looked like. But there was a difficulty. He was only a little man, the crowd was two or three deep and he couldn't see Jesus for the simple reason that he wasn't tall enough. He hurried up and down, trying to find an opening in the crowd, but when people saw who it was they bunched together and blocked his view. Then he had a brilliant idea. He ran on ahead and climbed a tree.

It's funny, isn't it?, that Luke's idea of what ought to go into his Gospel is in some respects quite different from ours. He doesn't give us any idea of what Jesus looked like, but he does tell us what the tree that Zacchaeus climbed up looked like. It was a sycomore. There's a difference between a sycamore and a sycomore. A sycamore (Acer Pseudo-platanus) is a kind of maple, and if it had been large enough to be climbed, its lowest branches would have been too high for Zacchaeus to reach. What Zacchaeus climbed was a sycomore (Ficus sycomorus), which is a kind of fig tree. It produces small, rounded figs that are more or less tasteless. In ancient times the apex of the fruit was sometimes pierced to hasten the ripening. Amos was a "nipper" of sycomore figs (Am 7:14). Mummy cases and many of the best preserved Egyptian wooden utensils are made of it.

Zacchaeus hadn't climbed a tree for years, and it was really rather difficult, but he got up eventually and sat on a branch with his legs dangling, looking completely ridiculous in his smart business suit. The crowd below started whistling and jeering, so much so that when Jesus arrived he looked up at the tree to see what everybody was laughing at.

Then Zacchaeus got the shock of his life. The teacher looked up and said: "Hullo, Zacchaeus, can I come to your house today?" They were just about the first civil words that anyone other than a tax-collector had addressed to him for forty years.

I don't suppose Zacchaeus ever got over the wonder of it. We can imagine him in after years saying to his friends: "There was Jesus, the Son of God, and he actually came to dinner in my house. Of course, I didn't know who he was then."

Non-believers stop here

What do you mean when you talk about 'my house'? You might be the person who owns it, though you don't actually live in it. You might be a tenant paying rent for it. You might be the person who built it, because if you've built something you always think of it as yours. If I drive round the South of Scotland I keep coming across one of my bridges.

So what about my life – or yours? Some people say: "It's mine; I can do what I like with it." That's true if you're the owner. But when you say: "It's mine", how did you get it? Did you buy it? Did you build it? It's obvious that you're a tenant, and a tenant can't do what he likes with a house. You furnished it, yes. It has some lovely, treasured things in it – most of them presents. Some of the things you've bought by experience, and often had to pay a heavy price for them. Some things are unpleasant, and we don't want other people to see them. Some we don't like to look at too closely ourselves, so we keep them in a dark cupboard.

The builder and owner of this life is God, and the worship we pay him and the love that we show for our fellow men and women are the rent that we pay for the life that is ours.

But Zacchaeus literally welcomed Jesus into his house. And it changed his life. A penniless man came into the house of a rich man and brought with him the only thing of any lasting value – love. He came in, sat at his table, ate his food and gave him love. If you really want to get to know someone that's the way to do it. Sit down and eat with them.

We don't know anything more about Zacchaeus. The last time we see him he's about to give half his belongings to the poor and pay back to the people he's cheated four times what he's taken from them. By the time he'd finished doing all that and finished settling his affairs, his new Master had probably been executed.

Then perhaps he heard from his old friend Levi/Matthew the amazing news that their Master was alive. I like to think of him hurrying up the road from Jericho to Jerusalem to join his new friends. It was a dangerous road, as we know, but he wouldn't worry about robbers; he had nothing left that they'd want to steal. The only thing of value that he had they could never steal.

His Master had come to his house, had a meal and left again. But he had also come into his <u>life</u> and now he'd never leave. And every time Christians meet for Holy Communion they know that they have their Master's promise that he'll come into <u>their</u> house and have a meal with them and never leave.

The Vine

<u>John 15: 1 – 8</u>

This is one of the occasions when it's important to use the right version of the Bible if you want to get the most out of a passage. Most modern translations tend to paraphrase the Greek rather than provide a literal translation. If a translator tries to paraphrase a text that he doesn't really understand he's liable to make mistakes. The translators of these modern versions may have been experts in biblical Greek, but they didn't know enough about vines.

Most modern language versions say: "Every branch that does bear fruit he prunes." But the King James Version says: "Every branch that beareth fruit, he purgeth it" and the New English Bible says: "Every fruiting branch he cleans." The Greek word translated by the King James Version as "purgeth" and by the New English Bible as "cleans" comes from the same root as catharsis, meaning cleansing or purifying. It doesn't mean pruning. When Jesus said: "The Father cleans the vine" that's what he meant.

Some years ago we moved into a house in Edinburgh which had a large, vigorous and very demanding vine in a greenhouse in the garden. It taught me a lot. It's the only plant I've ever come across which had to be cleaned regularly. It had to be pruned too, but that's a different matter and I'll come to that later. During the course of the year the branches developed a fibrous skin – you could hardly call it a bark. After a while the skin started to peal off, forming all sorts of nooks and crannies for insects and fungus, and unless you pulled off the skin the vine was unlikely to stay healthy. All our lives need cleaning, don't they? Gradually, often unconsciously, we surround ourselves with the dead husks of bad habits and outworn ideas. The habitual derogatory remark about people we don't much like. The enthusiasm which has withered into prejudice. The friendly rivalry which has darkened into bigotry. The dark corners whose very existence we try to conceal from other people and we prefer not to look at too closely ourselves. Some of these are quite painful to lose. Their loss leaves us tender and vulnerable. It's not always easy to recognise the hand of God, the husbandman, in the cleaning process.

Pruning, in the other hand, is quite a different matter. During the early summer the vine kept me very busy. In May the new shoots started growing incredibly quickly. I had to be continually pruning to prevent the vine from swamping itself with growth – to direct its energies to the production of fruit. Then, when the fruit had set, every bunch had to be drastically thinned so that each individual grape had room to swell and breathe.

Pruning is quite a different matter from cleaning. It's a matter of cutting away healthy growth, of channelling energy, of choosing priorities, of discipline. It may be a matter of restricting ones own activity so that others can grow. It's the process, for example, that all parents have to go through – often at considerable cost to themselves – the process of loosening the apron-strings so that their children can grow by being independent.

Of course, if the vine became less vigorous and productive there was less to do. Our vine had a trunk and three main branches. After some years one of the branches almost completely stopped producing fruit, so I cut it off and trained up a new young shoot to take its place. Within a couple of years it was the most vigorous and productive part of the vine. It's always the new, fresh growth that's the most vigorous and fruitful. Jesus said: "This is my blood of the new covenant." "I give you a new commandment, love one another." "Behold, I make all things new." And it's that spirit of newness that we must carry into our lives. It's got nothing to do with age. It's a readiness to let God's Holy Spirit cleanse us of all the old, dead ways that are only destructive of our spiritual health and fruitfulness. It's the fresh, vigorous growth that keeps the gardener, the husbandman, busy. And it's where Christ's disciples, the members of the true Vine, are most vigorous and fruitful that the Holy Spirit is most active.

The old branch that I'd cut out was useless and I threw it on my next bonfire. Which brings us back to Jesus' parable. "If anyone does not remain in me, he is like a branch that is thrown away and withers; such branches are picked up, thrown into the fire and burned." 2,500 years ago Ezekiel pointed out that vine wood is quite useless. You can't carve it. You can't even make a peg out of it to hang things on. You can't do anything with it but burn it. It exists to carry the life of the vine to the fruit.

If it stops doing that, if the sap no longer flows through it, it's fit for nothing but to be burned. And Jesus tells us that apart from him we can do nothing. All the fruit you and I can ever bear comes wholly from him, his very life-blood flowing through us. If we separate ourselves from him, if that life-blood stops flowing, the penalty comes immediately. Jesus isn't saying that if we don't abide in him we'll ultimately be thrown out of the vineyard on to the fire. This isn't a threat of damnation and hellfire at some time in the future. Our failure to abide in him is that rejection and destruction. Hell is self-imposed separation from God.

But there was one very important respect in which our vine differed from the sort of vine that Jesus was talking about. It had, as I said just now, a trunk with branches coming off it. But many of the vines that are grown for the production of grapes for wine have no trunks to speak of. They consist only of branches. Take away the branches and you take away the vine. There's nothing left. Jesus said: "I am the Vine, you are the branches." Everyone who is baptised is made a member of Christ – a member, a limb, of his body, a branch of the true Vine. We are the body of Christ.

It's an extraordinary analogy, this concept of the vine. Most analogies break down pretty quickly if you push them too hard. But this one is relevant to the human situation and our relationship with God in so many ways: cleansing, pruning, the fate of unfruitful branches, the relationship of branches to the whole plant. But above all, the most important attribute of the vine is that it produces fruit.

Non-believers stop here

At the Eucharist we bring the fruit of the vine and offer it to God. And we pray that he will send his Holy Spirit upon it and hallow it. But we bring, too, the fruit that we've borne as members, branches of the Vine that is Christ – the fruit of our daily life and work. And we offer that to God and pray that he will hallow it and use it in accordance with his will.

So the Offertory is far more than the presentation of the money that we've collected – more even than the offering of bread and wine. It's the offering of ourselves, our souls and bodies, our lives, our successes and our failures, knowing that

God will take them and hallow them and use them for his own good purposes. The bread and wine that we offer represent our offering of ourselves. They are for us exactly what they were for Jesus at the Last Supper – symbols of our bodies and our blood: symbols of ourselves. And at the Offertory, as St Augustine said: "There are you in the chalice."

Paradox at the Trial

Matthew 26: 59 – 68

Not for non-believers

It's strange that the Christian faith is riddled with paradoxes. Practically any aspect of it that you care to think of has its paradoxical side. The Son of Almighty God, whom the hosts of heaven worship and adore, born in a stable. The kingdom of God come upon us, here and now, so close we have only to reach out for it, but in another sense not yet, or why do we pray: "Your kingdom come"? The King of Glory enters his own city, riding on a donkey. His victory over sin won once for all on the Cross, yet, as we all well know, the struggle goes on.

Our very faith is paradoxical. It's rooted in doubt. In fact, faith can't exist without doubt. If you have no doubt you don't have faith, you know. Just as in the same way there can't be courage without fear. A man who is fearless doesn't need to be brave. Bravery is being afraid and going on in spite of fear. Faith is being doubtful and going on in spite of doubt. It's saying not: "I believe because . . ." but: "I believe in spite of . . ."

I find that an increase in age isn't necessarily accompanied by an increase in faith. I find myself in the same position as the man whose son was epileptic. You'll remember how Jesus' disciples tried to heal the boy but couldn't. The man appealed to Jesus and said: "If you can do anything, take pity on us and help us." "'If you can'?" said Jesus. "Everything is possible for him who believes." Immediately the boy's father exclaimed, "I do believe; help me overcome my unbelief." That's a prayer for most of us.

Paul wrote about another paradox in his first letter to the Corinthians – Christ crucified. No wonder the Jews found the idea a stumbling block. The Messiah who was going to lead his people and rule the world, executed as a common criminal. No wonder the Gentiles thought it foolishness. And Paul reiterates the paradoxical nature of his message. He talks about the divine folly – wiser than the wisdom of man; the divine weakness – stronger than man's strength. His point was that human wisdom is as nothing compared with the wisdom of God, so we must concentrate less on striving to reach God by our own unaided efforts, by our own wisdom. We must rely on faith. That's proved by the fact that: "God purposely chose what the world considers nonsense in order to shame the wise, and he chose what the world considers weak in order to shame the powerful. He chose what the world looks down on and despises and thinks is nothing, in order to destroy what the world thinks is important."

But I haven't mentioned so far what is perhaps the supreme, the most mysterious, the most holy paradox of the Gospel – he who was wholly God was also completely human. We find that very difficult. We're tempted to think that because Jesus was who he was it was easier for him to be good than it is for us. We're tempted to think that in some way he had certain privileges that are denied to us. It seems to me that the fact that that was not so is illustrated as well as anywhere in the story of his trial before the Sanhedrin.

It's paradoxical that at the very moment that Jesus was called upon to make his formal claim to be the Son of God we receive such convincing proof of his humanity.

As far as we know he's been silent throughout the hearing. All this business that Matthew describes, about his threatening to destroy the temple is irrelevant. He's not going to allow himself to be executed for that. But now the high priest uses legal terminology to compel him to answer. In the face of the formal demand: "I charge you under oath by the living God" Jesus must, by law, answer. Here comes the direct challenge: "Tell us if you are the Christ, the Son of God." He couldn't refuse to answer, even if he wanted to.

And what's the reaction to his reply? They spit in his face, they punch him, they humiliate him. That's not the way you treat a god. This is a man.

You can burn incense in front of a god; you can sacrifice to a god. You can keep it in a bank, if that's the kind of god you worship. But who ever heard of a god being treated like this? "Son of God" he'd said, but this is no pampered boss's son, working his way through his father's organisation, with everyone being nice to him because they know that one day he'll be the boss. I'm reminded of the story of the company chairman bringing his son into the factory for the first time to start work. "I want my son to start at the bottom and work his way up. Then after lunch . . ." There's nothing like that about Jesus. He is indeed about his Father's business, but he has no special privileges. This is a man.

And yet . . . Anyone who has seen him has seen the Father. Where this man is, God is. More than that – we have his promise: "I am with you always" so where man is – wherever any man or woman is – God is; in the depths of despair or degradation, on the heights of triumph and rejoicing. But perhaps more importantly for most of us, God is in the joys and sorrows, the fun and disappointments of everyday life.

The Gospels naturally concentrate almost entirely on the few short years of Jesus' ministry, and we're liable to forget that nearly all his life was probably as ordinary and humdrum as ours. He had to learn, as we all do, how to cope with the pressures, the pleasures, the frustrations of everyday life, and in doing so he sanctified the commonplace. His whole life was a sanctification of the commonplace, and at his death the veil of the temple was rent from top to bottom. The last barrier between God and man was down.

It's this breaking down of the barrier that we celebrate in the Eucharist. In the Eucharistic Prayer the priest says: "In Christ your Son our life and yours are brought together." At the Offertory we present to God not just bread and wine but ourselves, our souls and bodies, our humdrum lives, our little triumphs and defeats. And we believe that God accepts them and works his will on and through them. We can see the relevance of our everyday lives in the context of the Eucharist, and of the Eucharist in the context of our everyday lives. In the Eucharist, the holy paradox, the most ordinary things become the body and blood of Christ.

In the Eucharist, he who was fully human gives us his humanity in his body and blood so that our lives may be fulfilled. As children of the same Father we are his flesh and blood, and we can, and must, live life to the full as he did.

In the Eucharist, as in all our life, Christ sanctifies the commonplace. He takes a humble, simple action which is so commonplace that most of us do it every day, and makes himself known in the breaking of bread.

Barabbas

Mark 15: 6 – 15 (Matthew 27: 15 – 26, Luke 23: 13 - 25)

Barabbas was a robber. Then why should the crowd demand that Pilate should release him rather than Jesus? I think there are a number of possible reasons. We don't know much about Barabbas, but we do know that he was in prison following an insurrection. We can think of him as a leader of men – a demagogue. An attractive rogue with a wicked grin – a good public speaker who'd caught people's imagination. He'd led a revolt against the Roman occupying power. It had failed and he'd been arrested, but anyone who was prepared to rebel against the Romans was sure to be popular.

In the course of the revolt he'd paid off some old scores and murdered one or two people, but murder, strangely enough, has never been a bar to a sort of popularity. There have always been people who regard a murderer as a kind of public hero; people who are eager to listen to anything that he says; people who crowd to catch even a glimpse of him. Barabbas was like that. But since his arrest and imprisonment people had been looking for another leader, and they'd begun to wonder if Jesus of Nazareth was the man they were looking for. Only a few days ago he'd ridden into Jerusalem in a sort of triumphal procession, cheered by a crowd of yokels from Galilee, though he had rather spoilt it all by riding on a donkey.

And now there he was – a pathetic, lonely figure – looking nothing like a leader. And in any case there were some pretty tough-looking characters dotted about the crowd who were shouting for Barabbas. It might be better to keep on the right side of them.

So perhaps it's not surprising that the crowd chose Barabbas. You'll sometimes hear people talking about the fickleness of human nature; and one of their favourite examples is that the people who cried "Hosanna" on Palm Sunday cried "Crucify" four days later, but there's not a shred of evidence for that. The people who cried "Hosanna" were loyal Galileans, and it was they who during the next few days protected Jesus from arrest. During the Passover, visitors to Jerusalem outnumbered the local residents, but at night there weren't enough beds in Jerusalem to accommodate them, so they went and lodged in the surrounding villages – as Jesus and his disciples did. The crowd who shouted "Crucify" had gathered early in the morning, before the Galileans had come into the city. They were probably servants of the temple authorities, money-changers with a grievance, disgruntled dove-sellers, with a sprinkling of carefully placed rabble-rousers. Rent-a-crowd.

But what of Barabbas? We don't, as I say, know much about him, but we do know that his name seems to have had a special significance for the people who wrote the Gospels.

In some early versions of Matthew's Gospel he's called Jesus Barabbas. At that time the name Jesus or Joshua was quite common, so it's not impossible that Barabbas was called Jesus. By the time Matthew's Gospel was written the name Jesus was beginning to be related specifically to the Lord, so it's unlikely that Barabbas would have been called Jesus in the Gospel if that wasn't his name.

But there's more to it than that. Mark, in his Gospel, translates only two Hebrew words. He tells us that Bartimaeus means 'son of Timaeus', and he tells us that Jesus said 'Abba, Father'. Is it a coincidence, do you think?, that he's given us the meaning of Barabbas? It's 'Bar' – 'son of', 'Abba' – 'Father'. The son of the father – exactly the expression that

Christians use about Jesus in the Gloria in Excelsis at the Eucharist – 'Lord God, Lamb of God, Son of the Father'.

So the crowd outside Pilate's palace were presented with a choice between Jesus Christ, Son of the Father, and Jesus the robber, son of the father.

If you'd been in the crowd, which would you have chosen? I think they had a good excuse for choosing Barabbas. They knew him; he could talk; you felt your blood run hot with anger when he was speaking. He could fill you with hate for your oppressors, hate even for the people who disagreed with you. Jesus of Nazareth, on the other hand, was a countryman; they knew of him slightly, if at all. He only talked about love and the brotherhood of mankind. He hadn't even tried to defend himself. Yes, I can understand them choosing Barabbas. What's so hard to forgive is their shout "Crucify." After all, as Pilate said: "What evil had he done?" It's hard to forgive that shout. And yet he forgave them.

Non-believers stop here

And the choice is still there. On the one hand Jesus Christ, Jesus crucified, risen, alive, with us always to heal and strengthen us, to give us life – life in all its fullness. On the other hand Jesus Barabbas, treating all that as folly. Why be uncomfortable? Why not take the easy way? Grab what you can while you can. Grab the pleasure and the money and the self-indulgence. There's no guarantee that Barabbas' offer is a good one – knowing Barabbas it probably isn't – or that in any case it's more than temporary, but it certainly glitters and a lot of people accept it.

So which is it to be – Jesus the giver or Jesus the taker?

The Christian may think: "Yes, I see the contrast between the two appeals. I know that the difficult one leads to life and the easy one means death, but I made that choice long ago. I've been baptised and confirmed. I'm a committed Christian." But it's not quite as simple as that. After our Lord's temptation in the wilderness, the devil only left him for the time being. Barabbas, after all, is a robber and he's always liable to break in at times and in places where we least expect him.

So this isn't a once-for-all choice. We're continually being presented with this choice, and unfortunately we're liable to choose Barabbas without even realising what we've done. Or we agree with those round us because it's easier, and sometimes safer, to go with the crowd, not to be the odd one out. Making up our own minds and sticking to what we believe to be right can sometimes take courage. But the challenge faces us, as it so dramatically faced the crowd in front of Pilate, the challenge to choose <u>this</u> man, not Barabbas.

The Penitent Thief

<u>Luke 23: 39 – 43</u>

No one could have called him a good man. He was born in a back street in the slums of Jerusalem. He had an undisciplined childhood and became known to the police at an early age as a young tearaway. As he grew up he always seemed to be in bad company, always taking the easy way out, constantly yielding to the temptation to live at other people's expense. Soon he was wanted by the police for petty larceny. Every man's hand was against him and he found it best to get out of Jerusalem. Eventually he joined one of the gangs that made a living by ambushing travellers on the Jericho road.

But one day an ambush went wrong and two of them were caught. After that there could be only one end to the story, and early one Friday morning he and his mate were taken out of the city and crucified.

Some time later, through his agony, he was conscious that another victim was being brought to join them. He heard the sound of a cross being dragged over the ground, the murmur of voices, snatches of laughter, the orders of the centurion, a thud as the prisoner's feet were kicked from under him and he fell backwards on to the cross, the sound of hammer blows. And between the blows, the victim's voice – not screaming curses as he and his mate had done, but saying the last thing he could have expected: "Father, forgive them. They don't know what they're doing."

And what were they doing? The soldier with the hammer was simply obeying orders. This wasn't the pleasantest of jobs to be given, but he'd known worse. So he just got on with it without taking too much notice of the prisoner. He took no notice of what the prisoner said because he didn't understand Aramaic. He was a Roman, and he'd never taken the trouble to learn the outlandish language they spoke in these parts. We're rather like him in some respects – so much immersed in the day-to-day routine of our lives that we ignore the needs and worries, the uncertainties and the loneliness of the people round us. We don't want to understand when Christ speaks to us in the hungry and thirsty, the naked and the stranger, the sick and the prisoner. We don't want to understand when he says: "Seek first the kingdom of God." Jesus must have been thinking about folk like us when he quoted Isaiah who wrote about people who hear and hear without understanding. There's something of that soldier in us.

Then there was the centurion. He understood what the prisoner said, all right. Some hours later, when it was too late, he said: "Certainly this was a righteous man." But he was part of the Roman chain of command – subject to and imposing rigid discipline; a discipline that didn't require thought, only habitual obedience. Like the conscientious church-goer whose self-discipline brings him to church every Sunday without fail, but whose attendance at the service is so habitual that he finds it hard to concentrate on what's being said and done. It's fatally easy. I don't suppose I'm the only person who's realised to his dismay when it's too late that he's just said the whole of the Creed or the Lord's Prayer without thinking about it at all.

I'm not for one moment decrying the value of routine, especially the routine of going to church and reading the Bible and saying our prayers, but routine does have its dangers, and there's something of the centurion in each one of us.

Then there was Caiaphas, fighting to preserve his privileged position. Even rigging a trial and arranging for lying witnesses didn't look as if it were going to work so he played his trump card and compelled Jesus, as we've seen, to condemn himself out of his own mouth.

Our situation is very different from Caiaphas', but do we never abuse our privileged position? Perhaps being rude to a waiter or shop assistant who can't answer back, or bullying members of our own family who give in for the sake of peace. There's a bit of Caiaphas in most of us.

Then there was Pilate. I can't help feeling rather sorry for Pilate. All right, he was a weak man, he'd got where he was largely by influence, he wasn't up to the job he'd been given, but he was in a very difficult position. The Jews were an unruly lot who didn't take kindly to Roman domination. There'd been several uprisings in the past that had been difficult and expensive to deal with, and if there were another it wouldn't do his reputation in Rome any good. The country was especially plagued with religious fanatics, and it looked as if this were another one. He seemed harmless enough, but the priests had got their knives into him and the priests were uncomfortably influential. That nasty remark: "If you set him free you are no friend of Caesar's" was a very real threat. And after all he was there to keep the peace and wasn't the death of an obscure teacher from an obscure part of the province, miles from Jerusalem, let alone Rome, a small price to pay for keeping the peace and possibly saving many more lives?

And so the argument goes on until he persuades himself that this greatest of all evils is in fact the right thing to do. What would <u>you</u> have done? I think I'd have done the same as Pilate and persuaded myself that I was right. We spend a lot of time justifying ourselves for actions that deep down we know to be wrong. There's a lot of Pilate in all of us.

And what about the disciples? They don't really come into it, because at the first hint of trouble they ran away. And, God help us, who are we to condemn them? How many times have we failed to stand up for what is right and true? How many times have we failed to stand up and be counted as Christians? How many times have we kept quiet when we should have spoken out, for fear of contempt or ridicule?

It's a sorry tale. A tale of deafness and lack of understanding, of apathy and hypocrisy, of weakness and cowardice.

I'm reminded of that beautiful Negro spiritual "Where you there when they crucified my Lord?" It's a beautiful song, but it puts the blame in the wrong place, on to "them", whoever we may think "they" were. I think more appropriate words would have been: "Where were you when we crucified our Lord?"

A sorry tale, indeed. And if that were the end of the story it would leave us with an overwhelming burden of guilt. But that's not the end of the story. As we stoop under that burden we hear the voice of Jesus, saying: "Father, forgive them, they don't know what they're doing." The sorry tale is a tale of sorrow – of his sorrow for our sins, and he lifts the burden of guilt from us and carries it on the Cross.

. . . The hammering stopped, and a few moments later the third cross swung into the thief's view, with the inscription nailed to the top of it: "King of the Jews", and for the first time he was able to see his companion. And he recognised him. He'd gone down to Jericho one day to buy food for the gang and he'd found himself in the middle of a crowd of people who were pushing forward trying to see a teacher from Galilee whom everybody seemed to know about but him. As the teacher came past he caught sight of a little fat man who'd climbed up a tree to get a good view. The little man wasn't built for climbing trees and he looked ridiculous and knew it. And the teacher burst out laughing, but he wasn't laughing <u>at</u> the little fat men, he was laughing <u>with</u> him. The little man laughed, too. He scrambled down the tree and he and the teacher walked away together.

And now the teacher had met someone else on a tree, but he wasn't laughing now.

Jesus' road to Calvary had been very different from the thief's. He'd grown up in favour with God and man. His past three years had been full of conflict, but the conflict had resulted in a series of victories – victory over temptation, evil spirits, hypocrisy, even over fear of torture and death. Yet that succession of victories had inevitably led to Calvary.

And now he hangs beside the thief, helpless and defeated amid the jeers of the bystanders: "You saved others; save yourself." Even the other criminal joins in. And then the thief – also helpless – is surprised to find himself defending the teacher. He says to his mate: "Stop that. We got the same sentence as he did, but we deserved it. He's done nothing wrong." He turns his head to look at Jesus, sees him wearing his crown of thorns and says: "Lord, remember me when you come into your kingdom."

What a wonderful moment that must have been for Jesus! For hours, since early dawn, the cruel practical joke has gone on: Herod and his guard, the Roman soldiers, the people on the road, the bystanders. Here, at last, is sincerity. And it's rewarded by far more than the thief could have asked for. The supreme blessing that came to the dying thief was not only that his last moments were spent with Jesus but that he recognised him as King. And when Jesus' seeming defeat was revealed as victory the man whose whole life had been a succession of defeats was able to share in that final victory.

Non-believers stop here

And when we look critically at our own lives, and compare them, not with the thief's life but with our Lord's, we realise that there's not much to choose between us and the thief. In our shame we're tempted to say what Peter said when he didn't know Jesus very well: "Go away from me, Lord; I am a sinful man!" We want to hide. We don't want to think that God is with us. We don't want Jesus to turn and look at us. But thank God for the dying thief who, by the mercy of God, found his way to the kingdom by, so to speak, a short cut; and who became the first disciple to inherit the glorious destiny of all who acknowledge Jesus as Lord.

No short cuts for us, but we have something that the thief didn't have – time for amendment of life. And as each year we pass through Passiontide and Holy Week and prepare to share in the victory of the Cross and the triumph of Easter, may our prayer, too, be: "Lord, remember me", knowing that the answer will be: "Today, day by day, you will be with me."

Easter

Morning

John 20: 1 - 9

Caiaphas lay awake in the small hours of the morning and thought about the so-called prophet from Galilee. For the past two or three years he'd heard rumours of his activities and had wondered if there was going to be trouble. Eventually the man was foolish enough to come to Jerusalem at Passover time and had started to stir up the ignorant and the trouble-makers.

He'd claimed to be the Son of God – a blasphemy for which the penalty under Jewish law was death. But he'd also claimed to be a king, and Caiaphas had known that if the Roman Governor heard about that and took it seriously there would indeed be trouble. So he and the Council had got in first, and it was they who told the Governor. They'd violated all their convictions when they forced the Gentile oppressor to execute a son of Abraham, but they thought it was worth it.

Caiaphas had to admit that there had been something very disturbing about the man, but in the end he'd been a failure as they'd known he would be. After he'd been crucified someone had called out: "If you're the Son of God, come down from the cross." It had been a fair challenge, but it hadn't been accepted. By 3 o'clock it had all been over, and they'd been able to set about the task of purifying themselves in preparation for the feast. The episode was closed. Caiaphas smiled to himself. His triumph was complete. He turned over and went back to sleep.

On the other side of the city another man lay awake too. Peter was exhausted. He'd been up all Thursday night and since then he'd been too full of horror and self-disgust to be able even to relax, let alone sleep. For the past three years he'd followed a man who spoke as no other man had spoken. He'd believed that this man was the Messiah. He'd believed that the kingdom of heaven, the kingdom of love and peace, was at hand; and he'd been wrong. Jesus had saved others, but he couldn't save himself.

But even if he wasn't the Messiah he didn't deserve to die – let alone die like that. Peter had lost the best friend he'd ever had, and what made it worse was that he'd deserted Jesus at the very time he'd most needed someone to stand by him. At the very time that witnesses at his trial were telling lies about Jesus, Peter was telling lies about him, too; he'd denied all knowledge of him.

And on top of his overpowering sense of bereavement at the loss of his friend, on top of his disgust at his own cowardice, was a very real fear for his own safety. He wasn't only frightened – he was without hope. It was total disaster.

Triumph and disaster. The difference in the situations of Caiaphas and Peter could hardly have been greater. But one thing linked them. They were both wrong.

The Gospels are contradictory about the events of that morning. We'll never know just what happened, but we can get some feeling for the atmosphere. Outside the city the scene was much the same as it had been late on Friday night. The hill still loomed darkly against the night sky as two or three women approached the tomb. They had come to anoint their dead Master's body; there'd been no time to do it before the beginning of the Sabbath. But they were frightened, so they'd come early while no one was about. If they'd been spoken to their Galilean accent would have betrayed them, and all Galileans were suspect.

But someone had been at the tomb before them, because the first thing they noticed was that the stone blocking its mouth had been rolled away. We can imagine how frightened they must have been, wondering if someone was watching from the shadows. It must have taken great courage to go into the tomb. When they did, and when they discovered that the body was gone, that must have been the last straw.

And suddenly, on top of the sense of fear there's an added sense of urgency. Mary Magdalene turned round and ran – back into the city to the house where Peter and John were lodging. Peter and John ran back to the tomb. People seem gradually to have realised that something amazing had happened. The women were told that Jesus had been raised.

John saw the grave clothes and perhaps remembered the raising of Lazarus.

Lazarus came out of his tomb wrapped in grave clothes, with a cloth round his head. Jesus' grave clothes were lying in the tomb with the cloth that had been round his head lying separately. We don't know quite what John deduced from that – perhaps he concluded that the body had passed through the clothes, leaving them where they were. Whatever it was, John realised that there was something different here from what had happened to Lazarus. This wasn't just resuscitation. This was resurrection.

Emmaus

Luke 24: 13 - 35

That afternoon two of the disciples set out from Jerusalem to walk home to Emmaus. We don't know much about them. We know that one of them was called Cleopas and it seems almost certain that the other was his wife, Mary, because the two disciples obviously lived together at Emmaus and we know that Mary, the wife of Cleopas, was one of the women who had witnessed the crucifixion; so she had certainly been in Jerusalem. They must have had only one thing on their minds – the horrifying death of their Master. The two of them were so deep in conversation and so sunk in gloom that they hardly noticed the stranger who had joined them on the road until he asked them what the trouble was. They told him about the prophet Jesus of Nazareth, how they had hoped that he was the one who would redeem Israel, but how the chief priests had handed him over to the Roman authorities for execution. And then something remarkable happened.

Throughout the Gospels there are reported remarks or incidents which carry the stamp of authenticity simply because they are unexpected or funny or so unlikely that no one would have dared to invent them. Things that stuck in the minds of the people who witnessed them. Moments that make you think: "That's just how it must have been." This is an incident like that.

Jesus had risen from the dead only a matter of hours earlier. It was an event of awesome mystery which we can contemplate only with wonder and gratitude. It was an event of immeasurable significance, not only for himself but for all humankind. And he went to meet this couple. It's an encounter that will be remembered all down the centuries. A moment, you would think, of great solemnity. And almost the first thing he's reported to have said to them is: "You fools!" At first sight it seems an unlikely remark in those circumstances, but it's typical of Jesus.

The Gospels repeatedly report similar remarks and moments of exasperation. "How dull you are." "Fools." "Hypocrites" "Do you still not understand?" Repeatedly we are told that Jesus was angry. He was a man with a quick temper, or at least he found it difficult to be patient; particularly to be patient with people who wouldn't use their brains. He was a very human man. And this man talking to the two disciples is that same Jesus. The experience he's passed through in the previous three days hasn't altered his character. In spite of his death, in his new life he's still recognisably the same person – still quick-tempered, still impatient with people who are slow-witted.

The Bible tells us almost nothing about what life after death will be like. Knowing that we, his loved ones, will always be in God's love and care we don't need to concern ourselves with the details. But this little episode does provide confirmation that after death we'll still be identifiably the same person. And Jesus seems to have gone out of his way to prove to his disciples that he was the same by showing them his wounds and by eating with them.

So why didn't Cleopas and Mary recognise him? Luke says something prevented them, but we don't need to assume that any supernatural agency was at work here. They knew that Jesus had died. Mary had been there and seen it all. She probably saw the state he was in even before he was crucified. When it came to flogging a criminal Roman soldiers knew their job, and by the time they'd finished with him he couldn't even carry his cross. Mary may even have helped to take his body down from the cross.

So they knew he had died, and it would never for one moment have occurred to them that the man walking with them could possibly be Jesus. In any case, they were so wrapped up in their own distress that they probably barely noticed what he looked like.

It's a lesson to us, isn't it? When the going gets hard and troubles bear down on us, when there seems to be no escape, we are liable to wrap ourselves in such a thick layer of misery that we can't see out or see beyond it, and nobody else can get through to us. But it's just in these circumstances that Jesus himself draws near.

He may be there in someone who cheers us by the mere fact that they care. He may be there in someone who needs help. The best way to stop worrying about our own troubles is to start caring about somebody else's. He'll certainly be there, waiting to come into our hearts if only we will make him welcome. But we must see to it that nothing prevents us from recognising him – that we don't fail to see the unexpected.

So these three people get to Emmaus, and although Cleopas and Mary haven't recognised their companion, yet they are friendly, hospitable people and they invite the stranger to spend the night with them. "And while he was with them at the table, he took bread and said the blessing; then he broke it and handed it to them. And their eyes were opened and they recognised him." Even Jesus wasn't recognised in what he said, but in what he did.

But why should Cleopas and Mary recognise Jesus in the breaking of bread? Because neither of them had been at the Last Supper, when Jesus instituted the Eucharist. I think the answer must be that what they recognised was the familiarity of his movements – the way he performed the action of breaking the bread. Because they must have seen him do it so many times before at the Sabbath meal. The Sabbath meal was the inauguration of the Sabbath on a Friday night, and the first thing that happened was that the father of the family or the leader of the group took a piece of bread, said a short prayer of blessing, broke the bread and distributed the pieces to everyone at the table. That ritual was used on other occasions when a group of friends had a meal together, especially when a teacher had a meal with a group of his pupils or disciples.

At the end of the Sabbath meal there was another ceremony – the Cup of Blessing – when the father of the family or the leader of the group took a cup of wine and said a prayer of thanksgiving – in effect a solemn saying of grace. In the prayer he thanked God not only for the food and drink but for all the benefits he had bestowed on his people – for their liberation from Egypt, for the land they lived in, for his covenant with them and for the Law he had given them.

So when Jesus instituted the Eucharist at the Last Supper what he did must have been perfectly familiar to his disciples. They had seen him do it many times before. What was new wasn't what he did, but what he said: "This is my body which is given for you; this is my blood which is shed for you."

The Cup of Blessing had always reminded God's chosen people, the Jews, of their liberation from slavery in Egypt and of God's covenant with his people. Now it acquired a new meaning. It was to remind God's chosen people, the Church, of their liberation from the slavery of sin and of God's new covenant with all who follow Christ. Jesus said: "Do this. Break bread together; share the Cup of Blessing; do these familiar things <u>in remembrance of me</u>."

Non-believers stop here

And that's how it is for all Christians. We can, and should, say our prayers and go to church to worship God. Some people may even get up in a pulpit and try to proclaim the Gospel. But the whole business of being a Christian is not so much a matter of saying but of doing. Jesus' meat and drink was to <u>do</u> his Father's will, and his command to us is: "Follow me." And above all, of course, he left us something to do in the Eucharist. "Do this in remembrance of me."

Cleopas and Mary weren't important people. Cleopas wasn't one of the twelve disciples and after their return to Jerusalem we never hear of them again. They were just ordinary followers of Jesus, but they had the immense privilege of taking part in the first Eucharist celebrated after the Last Supper itself. Do you notice how similar it was to the Eucharist as we know it today? – the Eucharist that isn't just for apostles and great saints, but for ordinary, unimportant people like us.

It started with what amounted to a creed, modified only by the fact that they thought that their faith had been unjustified: "We had hoped that he was the one who was going to redeem Israel." It went on to the Liturgy of the Word, with Jesus expounding and explaining the scriptures. That was followed by the Liturgy of the Sacrament, with Jesus performing the four-fold actions of the Eucharist: He took, he gave thanks, he broke and he gave to them. But the most important similarity of all between that Eucharist and the Eucharist that we take part in today is that Jesus himself was the celebrant, as we believe he always is. He took ordinary, familiar things and hallowed them.

This hallowing of the familiar, of the everyday, is all of a piece with the Incarnation itself. The Incarnation isn't just the story of God made man, of the all powerful ruler of the universe entering the helplessness of a new-born baby, of him who made the world making furniture in a carpenter's shop. I say it isn't just that, though that in itself is staggering enough. The concept of the Incarnation is wider than that; it's the involvement of God in every aspect of human life. If our eyes are open we can recognise our Lord in the everyday things of life. But there's a danger here – the danger of over-familiarity. I suppose it's true for many of us that almost the only church service we ever come to is the Eucharist. We mustn't let familiarity breed, if not contempt, perhaps a lack of reverence. We must always remember that in the Eucharist we are handling holy things. We must never lose our sense of awe at the humility of God who is prepared to offer himself to us in this way.

But Christianity is full of contrasts and paradoxes, and here's another; because although we ought to approach the Eucharist with reverence and awe, that's only part of the story.

The word Eucharist is the Greek word for "Thank you." We talk about celebrating the Eucharist. This is a celebration of thanksgiving – a time of joy and gladness, foreshadowed by Isaiah when he said: "The Lord almighty will prepare a banquet."

You can't be solemn at a banquet. Have you ever noticed how many of Jesus' parables are about feasts and parties? He obviously enjoyed them, so it's natural that he should want us to enjoy the banquet that he has prepared for us. We may come burdened with worry, overcome with sadness, but remember Jesus at that first Eucharist. He must have been as apprehensive about what was going to happen to him, as frightened at the prospect of torture and death as anyone else would have been. He wouldn't have been human if he hadn't been scared. Yet if you read what he said to his disciples you'll see that it's full of references to joy.

So when we come to this celebration of thanksgiving let's be joyful. In the Holy Communion let's communicate – communicate our joy with the people near us. We are the people of God. All of us together. You can't have a banquet by yourself. And although, whether we recognise it or not, he is and always will be near us, yet supremely if we'll welcome him into our hearts and lives he'll be known to us in the breaking of bread.

Evening

Luke 24: 36 – 49 John 20: 19 - 23

It was almost dark, and Cleopas and Mary were hot and exhausted. They'd been hurrying for miles, desperate to get back into the city before the gates were shut for the night. They'd just made it, and now they'd got to the house and found the door locked. They were frightened of attracting the attention of unfriendly neighbours, so they tapped softly and when eventually someone came and they had identified themselves they were let in quickly and the door was locked again. Then they found that the news they'd brought – news that even now they could hardly believe – wasn't news at all.

The first thing that the people crowded into the room upstairs said was: "The Lord has risen!"

But with so many stories going round, most of the disciples didn't know what to think. Several women had been told that Jesus was alive. Mary Magdalene and Peter said that he'd appeared to them. The leg-weary disciples from Emmaus told their story.

Then . . . "Peace be with you" – and there he was. He'd come to his friends.

That triumphant resurrection might so easily have been a triumph over his enemies. The risen Lord might have appeared to Caiaphas, to the Sanhedrin, to Pilate. It would have been a spectacular revenge, but it would have done what Jesus had consistently refused to do. It would have compelled people to believe in him. Instead he appeared only to his friends – to people who already believed in him. To them he proclaimed the victory that he had won at Calvary, where the perfect man defeated the powers of evil. What Caiaphas and Peter had thought was defeat was just the opposite. In the garden on that first Easter morning, in the upper room that evening, he revealed the fullness of that victory. Now he had overcome not only evil but death. Now death could have no more dominion over him or his followers. It was the greatest victory the world has ever known.

Non-believers stop here

In that upper room Jesus offered his friends the gift of his peace – that peace which the world cannot give – and he sent them out into the world to live and work in his service. And all down the centuries since then Christian people have accepted that gift and tried to obey his commands. Jesus knew that life in the world would not be easy for us, but the victor of Calvary and Easter still comes to his friends as he promised he would; and he still sends them out into the world to live and work in his service. By his victory he's earned the right to say: "Take heart! I have overcome the world"; and we, his friends, can proclaim to the world the joyful message: "Jesus lives!"

Breakfast by the Lake

John 21: 1 - 17

Peter said: "I'm going out to fish." It's interesting that most of the experts who write commentaries on John's Gospel seem to agree that Peter and his six companions were guilty of apostasy, of giving up their faith, by going back home and taking up their old job as if they'd never met Jesus. I wonder if this is just a case of academics being experts in the New Testament, in Greek and Hebrew and theology and so on and forgetting about life. Maybe the reason that Peter and the rest went fishing was that they had to earn their living.

In the past few weeks they'd been through the most amazing experience. They'd been plunged into the depths of despair when their Master had been arrested and tried and executed and all their hopes had been shattered. Then they'd discovered in the most dramatic way possible that their Lord was no longer dead, he was alive. He'd met them and talked to them and blessed them and given them a job to do. From now onwards their lives would be transformed, but their lives still had to be lived. We know that a number of women supported Jesus and his disciples financially during his ministry. But now he'd died those funds somewhat naturally would have dried up. I think it's not unreasonable to suppose that until they could make other arrangements the disciples just had to go back to work.

Anyway, whether from financial necessity or not, there seven of them are in the boat together. But it's something like three years since they've been out fishing and perhaps in the mean time their luck or their skill has deserted them. Whatever the reason, they've been working all night and they've got nothing to show for it. And then, just as it's getting light a man calls out from the shore: "You haven't any fish, have you, lads?" "No" "Throw the net out to starboard and you'll catch some." Perhaps he's up on a bit of raised ground and can see the movement of fish more easily than they can close to the water. Out goes the net, and almost at once it's so full of fish that they can't pull it in, so they start to make for the shore, towing the net behind them.

The man's come down to the water's edge now and suddenly John says to Peter: "It's the Lord." Peter, impetuous as usual, can't wait for the boat to get in, but dives overboard and swims to the shore. What an unexpected reaction! Once before, when the Lord had helped him to catch a large haul of fish, Peter's reaction had been: "Depart from me, for I am a sinful man, O Lord", when he might have said: "Stay with me, and with your skill at finding fish and my skill at catching them we can build up a good business." This time, only a week or two after deserting his Master and denying that he knew him, Peter hurries to meet him.

I think most of us, if we're aware of having hurt someone or let them down, are reluctant to meet them and feel uncomfortable when we do. Not Peter, going to meet Jesus. But, of course, this wasn't their first meeting since that terrible Thursday night. Jesus had come to Peter on Easter Day. We don't know what happened at that meeting, but it's obvious from Peter's behaviour at the lakeside that having previously had an enormous weight of guilt and self-disgust on his shoulders he now felt himself completely forgiven.

When the rest of the disciples got to the shore none of them dared to ask the man who he was. They knew it was Jesus and that the mystical experience of the upper room on the evening of Easter Day was being repeated. They must have been filled with a feeling of awe, not knowing quite how to behave or what to say. And then Jesus said something that to my mind is about as unexpected as one could possibly have imagined. He said: "Come and have breakfast."

That hardy old perennial, the discussion about the physical resurrection of Jesus, keeps cropping up, but I don't see how the people who deny his physical resurrection can square their belief with this story, from which it seems to me that we must draw the conclusion that the only begotten Son of God, whom Christians acknowledge and worship as God from God, Light from Light, True God from True God, cooked the breakfast. This is a very down-to-earth religion we're involved with.

Then after breakfast there follows a remarkable conversation, on the face of it so cryptic as to be unlike anything else in the Gospels. Most English language versions of the Bible record Jesus as asking the same question three times: “Simon, son of John, do you love me?” and receiving the same reply each time: “Lord, you know that I love you.” The New English Bible does the same, but it also prints an alternative version:

> After breakfast, Jesus said to Simon Peter, ‘Simon son of John, do you love me more than they do?’ ‘Yes, Lord,’ he answered, ‘you know that I am your friend.’ ‘Then feed my lambs’, he said. A second time he asked, ‘Simon son of John, do you love me?’ ‘Yes, Lord, you know that I am your friend.’ ‘Then tend my sheep.’ A third time he said ‘Simon son of John, are you my friend?’ Peter was hurt that at the third asking he should have said, ‘Are you my friend?’ ‘Lord,’ he said, ‘you know everything; you know that I am your friend.’ Jesus said, ‘Feed my sheep.’

Hurt? He must have been heartbroken. He’d already denied his Lord three times and to his joy he’d been forgiven. Now he’s faced with denying him three times again. But when you’re face to face with God there’s no point in pretending and saying what you think he’d like to hear, so for the third time Peter’s answer comes back: “You know that I am your friend.”

But Jesus doesn’t leave it at that. He says: “Feed my sheep.” In effect, he’s saying: “I know that you don’t love me as I love you, but nevertheless I’ve got a job for you.” And we know that Peter accepted the job and that in the end he did what he said he would do on the night before his Lord’s crucifixion. You remember how he said: “Lord, I am ready to go to prison with you and to die with you.” He wasn’t ready then, though he thought he was, but now he’s abandoned his pride and his confidence in his own strength. And we know that he did finally face imprisonment and death in carrying out the job Jesus had given him.

Non-believers stop here

What an example Peter is to us. We've got so used to seeing pictures of saints in formalised positions with haloes round their heads that we're liable to forget that they were very human beings with all of our silly pride and weakness; and no one could be more human than Peter. Christians know that like him they've failed their Master, that after all their self-confident determination to stand by him they've run away when the going got tough. Like Peter they must learn that if they're ready to admit their failure their Lord is ready to forgive them, not just seven times but seventy times seven times.

But we can learn more than that from this story. One of the amazing things about the Gospels is their relevance to the present day. We can learn as much from what Jesus said and did as the disciples could.

For example, without Christ the disciples couldn't achieve anything. They'd worked all night and caught nothing. But directly they started following Jesus' commands the results were dramatic. Don't you feel sometimes that life's getting on top of you? There's so much you ought to do, that other people expect of you. You simply don't know how you're going to cope. Of course, in our own unaided strength we very often can't. But if we acknowledge that we need God's help he'll give us the strength to do what he wants us to do – which may not be what we want or expect. As Paul said: "I have strength for anything through him who gives me power." If we have the faith to rely on that gift the result can be dramatic. For the disciples the result was an enormous catch of fish.

One of the features of God's gifts is their extravagance. Do you remember Jesus' words: "Give, and gifts will be given you. Good measure, pressed down, shaken together and running over will be poured into your lap." The rewards for doing God's will are out of all proportion to what we deserve.

And then, Jesus called to the fishermen while they were at work. Have you ever noticed how often God speaks to people while they're working? Moses was tending sheep when God spoke to him from the burning bush. So was David when God sent Samuel to anoint him king. So was Amos when the Lord said: “Go and prophesy to my people Israel.” Simon and Andrew, James and John were working at their nets when Jesus called them to follow him. Matthew was at the tax office. All of them were going about their daily work when God called them. And we’re at least as likely to hear his voice when we’re going about our everyday humdrum lives as we are when we’re on our knees in prayer or sitting listening to a sermon, provided our ears and hearts are open.

And finally, the fishermen threw their nets out in response to a command from a man who obviously knew what he was talking about. If we respond in obedience to Jesus’ commands we can rely on the same thing. He’s earned the right to say: “Follow me’” to us as he did to Peter, because he knows from personal experience what it’s like to be human. Some non-Christians seem to have the impression that Christianity is an other-worldly, impractical exercise for people who enjoy being pious. But that’s a total misunderstanding of what Christians are about. Christianity is concerned with the worship and service of God who involves himself with every aspect of human life.

This is a very worldly religion because we follow a Master who knows from experience what it’s like to live in the world. All of us, I suppose, at one time or another live through times of tragedy and great sorrow, and other times of triumph and great rejoicing and happiness, just as the disciples did on Good Friday and Easter Day. But most of our lives aren’t like that. Most of the time we’re just carrying on, coping as best we can with the ups and downs of daily living. And it’s during those times – the ordinary, everyday, humdrum times – that we most need to remember that we’re invited to follow a Master who knows what it’s like to cook the breakfast.

Commissioning the Church

Ascension

Matthew 28: 16 – 20 Acts 1: 7 – 11

Thursday wouldn't be a good day for a public holiday. Perhaps that's why the secular world ignores Ascension Day and even the Church doesn't give it much prominence. The biggest congregations celebrate the joy of Christmas, the solemnity of Good Friday and the triumph of Easter, followed by the inspiration of Pentecost, but Ascension Day passes by almost unnoticed.

Yet the Ascension can be said to rank in importance with Easter. In the early Church, Jesus' resurrection and ascension were seen as different stages of the same event. But to see at any rate part of the reason why the Ascension is of such significance we have to go back to Christmas.

What an extraordinary event that first Christmas was! For centuries the Jews had been looking forward to the coming of the Son of David whom God would raise to be King. Yet when the Messiah came the event was both simpler and more dramatic than they could ever have expected. He wasn't born into a wealthy family. On the surface the only unusual thing about his birth was that his mother was away from home and had difficulty in finding accommodation. Yet Christians believe that that birth was the most awe-inspiring event that the world had ever known. Of all the prophets only Isaiah had had an inkling of what was to happen: "The virgin will be with child and will give birth to a son, and they will call him Immanuel", which Matthew tells us means "God with us." This wasn't just another prophet; this was a new King – Almighty God himself. God was with mankind. No wonder Christians throughout the centuries have celebrated his birth and year by year have sought to recapture the wonder of it.

So at Christmas we're presented with a mystery hidden in an ordinary, everyday event that anyone can understand; but the purely physical details of Jesus' ministry become progressively harder to comprehend, especially for people in the twenty-first century who expect to have a scientific explanation for everything.

Birth we've all experienced. Death we're going to experience, though I suppose most of us find that hard to accept. Even Jesus' resurrection – the concept of someone who was dead being alive again – is comprehensible if not physically explicable. But we've got no credible physical reference point to relate the Ascension to. The disciples told Luke what they'd seen, but as with the Transfiguration, they found no words to describe what was outside everyone's experience. In any case, they may not all have seen the same thing, or at least they may not all have perceived the same thing, just as people who are colour blind can't see things that other people take for granted.

What the disciples saw would depend on the depth of their faith, and Matthew tells us that "some doubted." And their description of what they saw would have been conditioned by their view of the world. They thought of the world as being essentially flat. Above it was heaven; below it was Sheol, the place of departed spirits. Between earth and heaven was the firmament, spreading over the earth like a dish cover. The disciples had read that Elijah was taken up by a whirlwind into heaven in a chariot of fire. So when Jesus was parted from them it was natural that they should look up.

The idea of heaven being 'up' has been perpetuated for us. "There's a friend for little children above the bright blue sky" as one of my least favourite hymns puts it. It's inevitable that we should think of heaven as being up, just as we think of anything superior being up. Children move up from one class to another. In most organisations people move up as they become more senior. There's no suggestion that it's meant literally and, provided that we're not foolish enough to believe that spacecraft have proved the non-existence of God, there's no harm in it.

But even the disciples got a warning that the idea of heaven being 'up there' mustn't be taken too literally. Two men in white said: "Why do you stand here looking into the sky?" That's not the way to find him.

But whether they heeded that warning or not, the disciples' idea of the nature of earth and heaven doesn't appear to have affected their faith. Their understanding of what they'd witnessed must have been clear and immediate, because although the cloud had removed Jesus from their sight they returned to Jerusalem with great joy. They'd lost him for ever, but they'd gained him for ever. They knew that life wasn't going to be easy for them. Jerusalem was the most dangerous place in the world for them. The religious and secular forces that had killed their Master would be only too ready to kill his servants. But they rejoiced not because he'd left them but because he'd never leave them. Never again need anyone say, as Martha said after the death of Lazarus: "If you'd been here my brother wouldn't have died." Now Christians know, as the disciples knew, that because he *is* here we will live. We'll live because in Christ our human nature has been taken up to God and accepted by God.

During his life on earth Jesus accepted the limitations inherent in being human. But he foresaw a time when through his disciples and his Church he'd overcome those limitations. Do you remember what he said? "Anyone who has faith in me will do what I have been doing. He will do even greater things than these, because I am going to the Father." In his final command before his Ascension he explained how that was to come about. He himself had brought the good news only to the Jews, but the disciples were to be his witnesses in Jerusalem, and in all Judea and Samaria, and to the ends of the earth.

Non-believers stop here

Because our Lord's first disciples obeyed his command to go and make disciples of all nations his good news has come to us. We've become his disciples, so his command is for us, too. We know, as the first disciples did, that the Gospel contains no promises that life is going to be easy. Being a Christian isn't a recipe for avoiding hardship and tragedy. On the contrary, being a Christian can still mean facing persecution and death. But our Lord's promise at his Ascension means that whatever the difficulties and dangers we don't face them alone, because the Gospel narrative starts and ends with the same mysterious, joyful message, though with a slight but all-important change of emphasis. The message of Christmas is: "God with us"; God is human. The message of the Ascension is: "God with us."

Pentecost

Acts 2

A few of the disciples got together that evening and tried to absorb what had happened and what it meant for them.

What a day it had been! The disciples had got into the habit of meeting early in the morning to break bread together, especially on the first day of the week, because that was the day on which the Lord had risen from the dead. They had to be early because the disciples who lived in Jerusalem had to be in time to get to work. The Galileans, of course, were so to speak on holiday. They'd stayed in Jerusalem because the Lord had told them to, but some of them must have been getting a bit worried, wondering how long they could spin out their money and when they were going to have to go home and get back to work. They'd be worried about their families, too, who'd probably have heard by this time that Jesus had been arrested and executed and would be wondering if his followers were also in trouble with the law and perhaps in prison or worse.

So they'd assembled as usual that morning. They didn't, in fact, have to be early because it was a public holiday – the Feast of Weeks, seven weeks and a day after the Sabbath at Passover time – so although it was the first day of the week most of them had the day off. It was the day on which the Jews commemorated the giving of the Law on Mount Horeb – a day they associated with wind and fire. And they'd remember how when Elijah long afterwards went to Horeb he experienced wind and earthquake and fire before he heard the still, small voice of God.

So there they were. There was an atmosphere of excitement and anticipation amongst the disciples. The Lord had said: "In a few days you'll be baptised with the Holy Spirit" so they knew that something was going to happen, though they couldn't think what.

And then it had happened – something that they were going to be asked to describe over and over again for the rest of their lives. But how can you describe a unique experience? If something happens which is unlike anything that's happened before, there can be no words to describe it. What they *could* say was that they suddenly became aware as never before that the good news that Jesus had brought was good news for people of every race and nationality, that it was their job to spread that good news, that the Lord who'd said that he'd always be with them would, in some mysterious way, help them to spread it and that the time to start was now.

They'd got so excited that a crowd collected, wanting to know what was going on. There were a lot of people about the streets with nothing much to do because of the holiday. I expect that then, as now, many of them took advantage of the holiday to spend a large part of the day in the pub; but everyone must have been a bit surprised to find a group of people who seemed to have started celebrating very early in the day.

Then there had been Peter's wonderful speech. What he'd said had moved the crowd so much that when he finished speaking the disciples had been almost overwhelmed by people wanting to know more about the Lord – about his teaching and death and resurrection. They'd ended by baptising no less than 3,000 people. Wasn't it lucky that it had been a holiday so that all the disciples were there to help?

Non-believers stop here

No, I don't think it was luck. It was one of the results of the Incarnation – of God becoming man, involving himself in every aspect of human existence. And God chose to baptise his people with his Holy Spirit not only on the first day of the week, but on this particular first day of the week when the people who received him were able to take full advantage of his coming.

Just as God the Son had subjected himself to the laws and customs of the society into which he was born, so God the Holy Spirit did the same thing. The Incarnation is a symbol of God's involvement with every aspect of the lives of each one of us – even our public holidays.

But all that had been earlier in the day. The crowds had gone away, the disciples had said goodnight to each other and dispersed. The local people had gone home; the Galileans had gone back to their lodgings. And you know what it's like when you've had an exciting and stimulating day. You've been to a wedding, perhaps, or a thrilling rugby international. You've been on your feet for most of the day. You're tired, but you can't relax. Everything seems a bit flat and for some reason rather depressing. For the disciples perhaps it's the first opportunity they've had to start thinking about the future.

A future in which they'll never again meet Jesus face to face. Never again hear him teaching on the hillside, by the lake, in the temple – never again see him healing people in the villages of Galilee. A future that for most of them will involve going home to their families, getting on with the humdrum business of living. A future in which everything will outwardly be the same as it always has been. Outwardly, yes, but in reality things will be very different, because that flame which alighted on them this morning will go on burning in their hearts for the rest of their lives if only they will allow it to do so. Though they can put it out if they want to.

So the future that those disciples – those first members of the Church – could look forward to was in some ways very like ours. We'll never walk with Jesus by the Sea of Galilee, never hear him telling stories. But at the same time we'll be spared the grief of seeing a man we love crucified.

As a festival, Pentecost doesn't seem to have the appeal to a wide body of Church people that the other great festivals have. We can rely on big congregations at Christmas and Easter, but Pentecost seems to attract less attention. Which is a pity, because if it hadn't been for that first Whitsunday the Church would never have spread beyond Jerusalem and before long would have died. But the people who heard the disciples speaking their own language were visitors to Jerusalem, and when they went home they took the good news with them and an extraordinary thing happened.

After the first reports of Jesus' resurrection started circulating in Jerusalem, the temple authorities must have been desperate to find his body, to prove that he was dead. They must have looked all over the place for it. But after Pentecost, wherever Christian folk met together, there was the body of Christ, springing up all over the place, proving not that he was dead but that he was alive.

I said just now that the future that those first members of the Church could look forward to was in some ways very like ours. So it was, but it was going to demand of them far greater courage than is demanded of most of us. You'll remember how Jesus had warned them that they'd be thrown out of the synagogues, and that would mean ostracism and probably unemployment. Their belief in Jesus as the Son of God would bring charges of blasphemy and might even lead to their death.

But in the quiet of that first Whitsunday evening, now that the excitement and the clamour had died away, they were left with the knowledge, the unshakeable conviction, that their Lord would always be with them and that his Holy Spirit would burn in their hearts for the rest of their lives. And the wonder of it is that if we'll allow it to do so that's as true for us as it was for them.

Lightning Source UK Ltd.
Milton Keynes UK
24 March 2010

151820UK00001B/41/P